The
BURG-O-RAMA
Man

By
Stephen Tchudi

dp
Delacorte Press / New York

Published by
Delacorte Press
1 Dag Hammarskjold Plaza
New York, N.Y. 10017

All of the characters and places in this book are
fictitious, and any resemblance to actual persons or
locations is purely coincidental. Of course, Burg-O-Rama
is fictitious too.

Manufactured in the United States of America

Designed by Elizabeth Fox

First printing

Library of Congress Cataloging in Publication Data

Tchudi, Stephen N.
The Burg-O-Rama man.

Summary: During the spring of Karen's senior
year the representative of a chain of fast food restaurants
and his camera crew choose five Crawford High School
students to feature in slice-of-life advertisements.
[1. School stories.   2. Advertising—Fiction.
3. Fast food restaurants—Fiction.   4. Restaurants,
lunch rooms, etc.—Fiction.]   I. Title.
PZ7.J9265Bu   1983   [Fic]   82–14075
ISBN 0–440–00833–6

For Emily, my number one reader and critic

CHAPTER 1

The first time I saw him was at a special assembly sometime late in February. I had been in Senior English, fourth hour, trying to figure out an odd-ball poem by William Blake, when the announcement came over the PA that the rest of the period was canceled. The entire student body shuffled into the big old barn of an auditorium that barely holds the 995 kids in Crawford High School. I looked around for somebody to sit with and spotted my best friend, Jane Heath. While we were scrambling for seats down front with the rest of the seniors, three people walked out onto the stage and took seats in front of the ratty-looking maroon curtain: Dr. McCollom, the principal; George Foley, president of the senior class; and this other guy—good-looking, probably in his early thirties, with dark curly hair.

"Who's that?" I asked, nudging Jane with my elbow.

"Dunno, Karen," she answered. "I've never seen him before."

"Cute," I said. "And nice clothes." The guy was wearing a dark suit with a vest, a light-blue shirt, and a sharp tie.

"Yeah, cute," Jane agreed, "but a little old, don't you think?"

"For me, maybe," I said, "but not for you."

Jane Heath is probably the most mature girl in the senior class—mentally, I mean, not just physically. She's a super student, the kind teachers call on when nobody else knows the answer, and she's in all the school service clubs. She is a shoo-in for the Good Citizenship Medal that the Daughters of the American Revolution give to the outstanding senior. But Jane is no goody-goody or grind or anything like that. She's fun outside of school, and because she is really attractive, she is always in demand for social activities. When I say she's mature, though, it's mainly because unlike a lot of pretty girls around Crawford High, she doesn't try to use her looks to get anywhere, with kids or with teachers.

"Well," Jane said, nodding toward the stage, "it looks like we're about to find out who he is."

At that moment George Foley was walking to the microphone on the stage. I always kind of laugh at George when he's up there, even though he's another one of my good friends. He always looks very serious about his duties as senior class president. Now he glared out at the crowd and waited for the freshmen in the balcony to quiet down. Then, still looking more serious than he ever did when he was with the rest of us, he led us all in the Pledge of Allegiance, his hand over his heart, staring at the flag that stood in its painted gold stand at the edge of the stage.

After the pledge George paused for a moment and then spoke again.

"Fellow students," he said, his voice electronically rich as it came through the speakers, "I present our principal, Dr. Benjamin McCollom." As George admitted, that was a silly thing to say, since everybody in the place knew who Dr. McCollom was, and he needed no introduction.

Dr. McCollom stepped to the microphone and started to speak, but the amplifier system made a great high-pitched howl. He stepped back and made a face, and everybody laughed. McCollom is popular with the students. He's fair about discipline and seems to care about how every kid in the school is doing.

"Good morning," he said, after adjusting the microphone, and a few people said "Good morning" back.

"We have a special guest today who will tell you about an exciting program that will be conducted here at Crawford. I'd like you to meet Robert Leseney, who is a representative of Trimble Enterprises, Incorporated." Dr. McCollom paused and looked at the guest. "And with that, I'll turn the platform over to Mr. Leseney."

Robert Leseney seemed a very confident man as he approached the microphone, and as he scanned the crowd, I wondered whether his curly hair was natural. He sure looked like the sort of guy who went to a stylist, not to an ordinary barber.

"How many of you kids have eaten at a Burg-O-Rama restaurant?" he began, and every hand in the place went up, mine included. There is a Burg-O-Rama out at the mall, and everybody in Crawford City eats there once in a while.

"Well," he continued, "Trimble Enterprises, the company for which I work, is the owner and exclusive franchiser of Burg-O-Rama restaurants." A cheer went up from someplace in the auditorium, and people laughed. So did Robert Leseney.

"I hope that you have seen our commercials on TV," he went on. "You may know that our ads feature a technique that is known in the advertising trade as slice-of-life. As far as possible, we use real people, not actors and actresses. People caught in the act of being natural. And of course, people caught in the act of enjoying our delicious foods."

He smiled, and a few people laughed with him.

I had seen those ads. They were filled with pictures of people of all ages doing things: throwing Frisbees, walking dogs, riding bicycles or jogging, singing songs. The people were always having a good time, and there would be shots of them chowing down burgers and fries, while the Burg-O-Rama theme song was playing in the background. The commercials were not only catchy, they made you feel good about life.

"The news I have today," he said, "is that we are going to do a new series of slice-of-life commercials." The auditorium was silent. "A series of commercials filmed right here in Crawford City." People started to mutter. "Filmed here in the halls of Crawford High School." A terrific gasp went up and everybody started talking out loud.

Mr. Leseney waited for the hubbub to die down, which it didn't, at first. "And . . ." he said into the microphone to catch our attention. "And . . . and . . . some of you will be the stars of those commercials."

Now there was an uproar. Who could tell a bunch of high school kids they're going to be stars in television commercials without provoking a pretty violent reaction? It seemed a long time before he could get people quieted down again. He got help from George Foley, who stood up and motioned for silence, palms down—keep the lid on.

"Here's how it will work," Robert Leseney said when order had been restored. "For the next month I will have a camera crew here at school. My cameraman will be in many of your classes, in the halls, in the cafeteria, at sporting events, filming people." As kids turned in their seats and excitedly started jabbering he made a motion just like George had—pushing monkeys back into a barrel. *"Pay no attention to him.* Don't wave at the camera; don't look at the camera. Just go about your business as usual."

People talked that over and he waited for silence.

"Eventually," he continued, "we will select five people from the school who have interested us, and we'll edit the film and make a slice-of-life profile of them. We'll also ask them to come over to Burg-O-Rama for a meal—on us, of course." He laughed, and so did we. "And we'll film them at the restaurant and add that to their profile. These profiles will be our new national commercials."

He clasped his hands. "But there's more." He paused for a moment as if thinking. "Are you kids interested in earning money?" This guy knew how to turn on a crowd. Half the students shouted back, "Yes!"

"The people who star in our commercials will be paid. For their work they'll receive what's called Actors' Equity rate. This means an initial fee for appearing in the commercials, and in addition, every time a commercial is shown, they will be paid a bit of money called a residual."

There was murmuring in the crowd as people wondered to themselves and one another how much money.

Robert Leseney had the answer. "Now I cannot

and will not make any promises, but you should know that it is possible for an actor or actress to make ten to twenty thousand dollars for this kind of commercial filming."

The place went up for grabs again.

"And . . . and . . ." Mr. Leseney waited. "And . . . in addition, through a special agreement with the Crawford City Board of Education, Burg-O-Rama, Incorporated, will also make a contribution to the school system for development of educational programs."

Who cared? Everyone was excited about the possibility of making a personal fortune.

"We have chosen . . . We have chosen . . . Burg-O-Rama has selected Crawford City, Ohio, and Crawford High for their representativeness of middle America. We think you are *the* typical community, *the* typical school, and *the* typical students in America today." He looked us over as if to see if he was right.

"I will look forward to working with you." Then Robert Leseney waved and walked back to his seat. The students gave him a thunderous ovation.

And after that day we never called him anything but the Burg-O-Rama Man.

"Amazing," I said to Jane Heath as we pushed our way out of the auditorium. "Simply amazing."

"What? The deal? The guy?"

"The whole thing. Amazing that Burg-O-Rama

somehow found Crawford City, tucked away in the back woods of southern Ohio."

"Yeah."

"And amazing to think of what this is going to do for our senior year. There's going to be some excitement around here for a change. I may even have something to write about for the *Tiger Eye*."

Jane laughed. "Ah, yes. I see that look in your eye. Karen Wexler, ace reporter. Get out your note pad, kid, and go track him down—that Burg-O-Rama Man."

"Well, not right away," I said, but she had me dead to rights. I'm editor of the Crawford *Tiger Eye*, a weekly four-page rag that I put out almost single-handedly, except for some help from a few sophomore journalism students, most of whom don't know a pica stick from a ten-point rule. I'm always running around looking for news, and my first reaction to just about everything that happens is to see if I can turn it into a story. "But before I try for an interview with him," I said, "I'll start a story about students' reactions. Maybe beginning with an interview with the Power Mongers over lunch."

The bell rang just as we reached the door of the auditorium—end of fourth hour, beginning of fifth, and by happy circumstance, lunch hour—so Jane and I went off to find our group of friends called the Power Mongers.

They call us that—the underclassmen do—

because every member of the group is a captain or a president or in charge of something around the school. I'm included because of the school paper —though I don't see quite why since nobody around school pays much attention to what I write anyway. Jane Heath is in because she's so busy with clubs and everybody knows she'll be voted "most likely to succeed."

George Foley is another of the Mongers, not only because he is senior class president, but because he's a good athlete—football and baseball— and sports are very, very big around Crawford. George is also just plain fun to be with, and that's why he's so popular and probably why he was president of our class freshman, sophomore, and junior years too.

The other two members of the group are Tom Garver, football captain and all-around handsome guy, and his girl friend, Kelly Flynn, blond, cute, and captain of the cheerleaders. Around Crawford kids say that Kelly and Tom's relationship was made in the stars. I don't know about that, but they're practically inseparable and have been that way for four years, even when Tom was freshman quarterback on the junior varsity football team and Kelly was the only freshman on the JV cheerleaders. I've always enjoyed being around Tom because he's relaxed and good-natured. Kelly, though, I could do without. She knows she's pretty and thinks her looks will get her anything she wants. As a matter of fact, so far in life her looks probably *have*, but it hasn't done much for her personality. She can't stand not to be the center of attention, and if you say anything that she thinks is even slightly negative about her, she either gets really nasty or goes into a sulk.

The Power Mongers are one of my chief sources of news for the *Tiger Eye*. They not only know what's happening, they *are* what's happening. If there's a dance or a pep rally, Kelly plans it; if it's a club activity, Jane's in charge; and if it has to do with sports or politics, Tom and George do it.

After the assembly Jane and I headed for the cafeteria. I checked the standard menu, which highlighted a sloppy combination of elbow mac-aroni, ground-up hamburger, and stewed toma-toes, and went through the à la carte line. I bypassed pizza slices, which is what I really wanted, in favor of an apple and a banana. Jane, who can eat anything and still keep in shape, bought a couple of tacos.

We found the Mongers' regular table and pulled up chairs. The rest of the group was al-ready there, George gulping down one of his two grilled cheese sandwiches, Tom and Kelly with their heads together talking quietly, feasting on love and letting the Sloppy Joe they would share get cold.

"So, what's new with you people?" I asked, and they all three looked up.

"Oh, hi, Karen," George Foley said. "I was just thinking about organizing a pool."

"I said what's *new*, Foley. You're always organizing pools."

And he is. I predict that George will become a professional gambler when he gets older. He'll bet on anything. I tease him and say that if he sees an old lady crossing the street, instead of helping her, he'll start a pool on whether she makes it to the other side.

George gave me a sour look. "This pool *is* new. I'll let you guess what students will be chosen to star in the Burg-O-Rama commercials. You can get into the pool for a dime."

"A dime for what?"

"A dime for a name. You put in ten cents and write the name of the person you think will be selected. The five people who pick the right names split the pot."

"I think it's a dumb pool," said Kelly Flynn. "I don't see how you could ever guess." Why did Kelly always have to play the dumb blond?

"Sure, the odds are small," George said, "but it's only a dime."

"That's throwing away your dime," Jane Heath said, practical as usual.

"Can you enter more than once?" I asked.

"Sure," George said. "In fact, you could improve your odds by betting on several people."

"Right," I agreed. I did some quick mental

arithmetic. "As a matter of fact, George, I know how to improve the odds so I can beat your pool."

"How's that?" George was hurt. He likes his games to be foolproof, or else rigged so that only he can win.

"Simple. I will bet a dime on every kid in the school. That way I can't lose. In fact, I will win all the money, including my original investment. I'll clean you out."

"Damn," George said. "She's right. The deal's off." He turned over a cheese sandwich on his paper plate and looked at it grumpily, as if he'd find a better idea written on the other side.

"But along the lines of the Burg-O-Rama thing," I said, "I'd like to gather some student opinions for next week's paper. Who better to interview than you four?"

"None better," said George, lifting his chin out of his sandwich. George loves to be interviewed and get his name in print. He doesn't read the articles, of course, just looks for his name.

"Who are the most likely candidates to become TV stars?" I asked.

Jane patted Tom Garver on the shoulder. "Tom, of course. It seems to me that he has as good a chance as any of us here. He's important around school and in sports and would look terrific on television."

One thing I've never figured out about Jane is why she has a crush on Tom Garver. She's always liked him, and she is absolutely not shy about praising him in public, even when Kelly Flynn is around. Kelly's got Tom all sewed up, of course, and Jane knows that. She doesn't make a fool of herself chasing him or anything like that, but I just don't understand why Jane pours so much praise on him.

"It probably won't be me," Tom said, though I sensed he hoped it would be. He turned away from Jane and held up Kelly's hand, which he had been holding under the table. "I think it has to be Kelly," he said. "I don't see how the Burg-O-Rama Man could miss her."

Kelly smiled back happily, and you could see she believed him.

"Right," I said, and seeing a chance to puncture Kelly's smugness, I added, "I'd bet a dime on her any day."

Kelly glowered at me, but no smart reply sprang to her glossy lips.

"And who else?" I put in fast before Kelly could gather her wits.

"I can't think of anyone," Tom answered.

"Me neither," Kelly added sullenly.

I sighed. Those two didn't seem to realize there was anyone else in the school except them. It was too bad Tom was so stuck on Kelly; Jane would have been a lot better for him.

"Well," I said, pulling a note pad out of my purse and shifting my gears into *reporter*, "Let me ask you another question then. Do you think it's a good idea for the commercials to be filmed here?"

"Yeah, it's terrific," Tom said.

I couldn't quote something as simple as that, so I looked around, hoping somebody would say more.

George cleared his throat. "I think it is a great opportunity for the school," he said. "It is a very positive reflection on Crawford High School and its students." He was trying to sound like the senior class president. Quotable. But I wrote it down anyway, thinking I might not get anything better.

"But what about the distraction?" I asked, with my pencil poised to write. "Like, what do you think of the commotion of having a camera crew around. Won't that interrupt our studies?"

They all four laughed.

"I can't quote that," I said, smiling too, "but I sense you do not see that as a major concern." Sometimes I sound quotable to myself. Once George Foley said I should stop acting like a TV reporter and be one of the gang a bit more. Maybe he was right. But I take my newspaper seriously. I don't have a "TEEN TATTLINGS" gossip column or some of that other junk I've seen in high school papers: "SOPHOMORE SIGHS," "MYSTERY TEACHER," "GUESS WHO?" baby photos. I try to stick to real news. Still, maybe George is right and I should try to lighten up.

"Filming would not bother me," Jane said. "I'm not learning anything now. . . . Especially in Pinnavia's history class."

"Which we gotta go to shortly," Kelly said, looking up at the cafeteria clock.

Pinnavia is the worst teacher in the school. He can't remember anything—his notes, the assignments, the dates of the Spanish-American War. The students have to help him out a lot or the class would become completely disorganized.

"For sure they won't film in his class," Tom said. "It would be too boring." He pushed back his chair and, still holding Kelly's hand, started to help her to her feet.

"Wait," I said. "Don't go just yet. I don't have what I need for a story. Don't you guys have anything else to say about the Burg-O-Rama thing?"

Jane tried to help me out. "I think it will be great for the kids who get chosen and make all that money. And great for the school too. Remember, he said the school will get some money."

"I remember," I said. "New books for history class, maybe."

People groaned, and Kelly checked the clock again.

"If you'd like to know," George said suddenly, "I think one part of the whole deal is very unfair."

"I'd like to know," I said.

"I think it's not fair that only five kids get the money."

"Right," Kelly agreed.

"Actually," George continued, "I think it would be a good idea if the money was pooled and everybody got a share of it. I think I'll propose that to Dr. McCollom."

I did some more figuring in my head. "If the money came to $15,000 per lucky kid and was split 995 ways, that would come to about $75 for each person in the school."

"Neat," Kelly said. "That would be great!"

Jane disagreed. "That would be ridiculous. $75 wouldn't mean anything to anybody. But with ten or fifteen thousand, those kids can do something, go to school, or maybe invest in something."

"That's true," George said quietly. It was not a good day for him and his ideas.

"Do you want to know what I think?" I said, since nobody had asked me. Nobody ever interviews the editor.

"Yeah," Tom said, without enthusiasm.

"I'm bothered by something else."

"Which is?" George asked.

"The way the Burg-O-Rama Man kept talking about us as *typical*. *Typical* students, a *typical* school, a *typical* town. I personally don't feel all that typical, and I think it's kind of insulting."

"But Karen, maybe that's just a gimmick," Jane said. "You know that everybody thinks that the Midwest, especially Ohio, is typical or average."

"I would think," I replied, "that in those commercials they would want *un*typical people. People with flash and style. Go-getters. Up-and-at-'em types."

"Like Kelly," Tom said.

"Like Kelly," I agreed reluctantly. "Or Jane," I added, to even things up. "But the point is, the average person would look dull on the screen. Who cares about average, typical people anyway? I think maybe they should say that Crawford was chosen because it is *a*typical, *un*usual, *not* filled with run-of-the-mill Ohio kids."

I thought for a moment.

"In fact, I think that will be my story, done as an editorial. 'HOW TYPICAL ARE WE?' Folks, you've given me what I came for. Thanks."

The bell rang for the end of lunch hour.

"It's time," Jane said. "Let's go wake up Pinnavia."

Kelly stood up, gave her tail a wag, and headed for the door in some sort of cheerleader strut. Tom and George followed her out, looking kind of foolish, and Jane and I brought up the rear.

There we went. Five typical teen-agers from a typical school having finished a typical lunch and off to a typically boring history class.

I don't know exactly why I was so bothered about that "typical" stuff, but Crawford City is a pretty nice town to come from, in my opinion, not just another spot on the map. Like a lot of places named "city," Crawford really isn't one—the population is only about seventeen thousand. The downtown area is an old-fashioned town square with a bandstand and Civil War monument in the middle. The Morgan County courthouse is on the west side of the square. Junius P. Crawford High School, named after our founding father—a guy who opened a mill on the Morgan River over a hundred years ago—is on the south. The other two sides of the square are bounded by U.S. Route 68, which makes a turn in Crawford City before heading out of town. There are a number of small stores and shops on those other two sides: a hardware store, a clothing store, two insurance agencies, a couple of banks, and the Stop 'N' Snack luncheonette. In the past few years a lot of Crawford's actual business has moved out to the new shopping mall. In fact, except when there are high school kids around, the downtown is dead.

However, when word got around that the Burg-O-Rama Man was coming, there was a lot of discussion about what the commercials would do for the town's image. The Crawford *Sentinel* ran an editorial saying that this could lead to a "resurgence of interest" in the downtown shopping area, though I couldn't quite understand how, and the mayor issued a proclamation of welcome for Mr. Leseney and Trimble Enterprises.

About the only person who didn't think the Burg-O-Rama commercials were a good idea was

Mrs. Greene, the mother of a boy in the junior class. She wrote a letter to the *Sentinel* saying that Burg-O-Rama sold nothing more than junk food and that the town shouldn't let the school be used for filming the commercials. She said that the school board "should not let commercial interests exploit our young people."

The Burg-O-Rama Man saw her letter and wrote a reply that appeared a day or two later. His letter said that since only those kids whose parents approved of them being in the commercials would be chosen, there was no danger of anybody being taken advantage of. He added that he "took serious issue" with Mrs. Greene over the term "junk food," that Burg-O-Rama hamburgers met all U.S. government standards and were 100% natural, not junk.

I asked a few kids around school what they thought of Mrs. Greene's letter, but most hadn't read it or just thought that she was crazy or a crab.

"Is that Bobby Greene's mother?" asked Kelly Flynn.

"Yeah, I think so."

"It figures," she said, making a face. "Bobby's a cute guy, but he never gets to do anything."

Within a week the Burg-O-Rama Man brought his film crew to school. As a matter of fact, the "crew" consisted of only one guy, a chunky man, probably in his late twenties, who we named the Big Fella, after Burg-O-Rama's half-pounder (with lettuce, tomato, onion, pickles, catsup, and mayo stuffed in a sesame bun). The Big Fella walked—almost waddled—around the building with a couple of leather camera-bags slung around his neck. He carried a big camera with a shoulder rest that he had wrapped in hospital-type adhesive tape, all brown and tattered from use.

The Big Fella wasn't clumsy, though, not at all. Even carrying around all that junk, he could ease his way down an aisle or through a corridor without hitting anybody. He never said anything to us, and when he was filming, he looked very serious—almost angry—so nobody said anything to him either.

The first day of the filming we had a short assembly, a twenty-minute job, right in the middle of second period. That was a drag because I have gym second hour, and that left just twenty minutes to change into gym clothes, play volleyball for about five minutes, then shower and change back. The changing was more of a workout than the volleyball.

Because it was a short assembly, George Foley didn't have to lead us in the pledge. Dr. McCollom was there, but he stood in the wings, watching. The Burg-O-Rama Man and the Big Fella were the whole show.

First the Burg-O-Rama Man introduced the Big

Fella, whose real name was Kenneth Deitrick. He had been the photographer for all the other Burg-O-Rama commercials, and the Burg-O-Rama Man said he was absolutely the best man in the business, a real artist and craftsman.

Then he spoke to us. "You remember last week I told you I didn't want you to wave your hands or look at the camera?"

"Yes," some people remembered out loud.

"Well, just in case you still have an urge to do that, I want you to get it out of your system. In just a moment, Ken Deitrick will shoot some film of the entire student body."

He motioned to the Big Fella, who shouldered his camera.

"Now . . . wave!"

Everybody waved like mad.

"Say 'Cheese' . . . and give me a big smile."

We grinned like happy Swiss cheese makers.

"Yell 'Hello-o-o-o!' "

"Hello-o-o-o!"

The Big Fella panned his camera back and forth, starting in the front where the seniors usually sit, then working up to the balcony and the freshmen.

"Thank you," said the Burg-O-Rama Man. "Now let me tell you how we are going to use that footage."

He leaned over the microphone.

"We plan to do one commercial to introduce

this campaign to the general public. We'll show shots of the school and the town, and we'll explain that we are going to highlight Crawford in our advertising. And we'll use the film we've just shot to show the entire student body waving a big hello to all of America."

With that the Burg-O-Rama Man and the Big Fella gave *us* a wave and headed offstage, shaking hands with Dr. McCollom as they left. We gave them another ovation for their troubles.

The Burg-O-Rama Man and the Big Fella spent the whole month of March around the school, but the commercials didn't actually begin to appear on television for a couple of months after that. We were told that all the film had to be edited and the background music piped in. Several different versions of each commercial would be shown to test audiences someplace else to see how people would react. Then, finally, the first commercial came out, announcing the whole series to the public just as the Burg-O-Rama Man said it would.

◆ ◆ ◆

OPENING SHOT: Morgan County courthouse at sunset, silhouetted against the sky, with flashes of sunlight bouncing off the dome.

ANNOUNCER: This is Crawford City, Ohio, U.S.A.

SHOTS (in quick succession): Old woman pushing a baby carriage, telephone lineman in a hard hat, young child with tricycle stuck in the mud, druggist talking to a customer.

MUSIC: Burg-O-Rama theme hummed softly by a chorus with orchestra backup.

ANNOUNCER: It is a typical small midwestern town, a happy place to live, work, and play.

SHOTS: Close-up details of buildings: old houses and modern, downtown stores, and boutiques at the mall.

MUSIC: Orchestra shifts from violins to electric guitar, from mellow strains to gently driving rock 'n' roll.

ANNOUNCER: You'll be seeing some of the people of Crawford City in coming weeks and months. They are part of the Burg-O-Rama family.

SHOT: The Crawford City Burg-O-Rama. Camera zooms in, looking through the front window, to pick up the faces of people inside.

MUSIC: Beat grows more intense. Chorus sings the lyrics of the Burg-O-Rama theme:

> *Burg-O-Rama, what a treat!*
> *It's the place for you to eat.*
> *Burgers, fries, and soft drinks, too.*
> *Burg-O-Rama's the place for you.*

ANNOUNCER: Now we want you to meet some more of the fine citizens of Crawford City, the people of Crawford High School.

MUSIC: Cymbal crashes. Music turns to a march beat, sounding like a school fight song.

SHOTS: The school from across the street, followed by a rapid sequence of close-ups: the main corridor, the cafeteria line, a drinking fountain, the door to the auditorium. Then students: a mix of faces, arms, blue-jeaned legs, and sneakered feet.

ANNOUNCER: We'll highlight them in future messages, and now they join us in giving you a great big hello.

SHOT: The student body in the auditorium, waving. "Hello-o-o-o!" heard over the music.

MUSIC: Swells to finish.

SHOT: A glowing Burg-O-Rama symbol fills the screen, then shrinks to the upper left corner. A written announcement appears:

> A promotional fee has been paid to the Crawford City, Ohio, Public Schools by the Burg-O-Rama Foundation, a division of Trimble Enterprises, Inc.

◆ ◆ ◆

It was beautiful. It was hokey, too, but it was beautiful. The Big Fella *was* an art photographer. Every picture in the film was one you could frame, even the ones of people eating. You couldn't help but feel proud, even with that stuff about being part of the Burg-O-Rama family.

As I learned later, that "family" is pretty big. Trimble Enterprises is into just about everything

—from bug bombs (Out!) to vacuum cleaners
(Sani-Sweep). They also make crackers (Taco
Taste), laundry detergent (Rinse Away Blue),
and soft drinks (Frostypop, the only kind you can
buy at a Burg-O-Rama). The Crawford City Burg-
O-Rama is one of two thousand in the fifty states,
plus a handful in Puerto Rico, the Virgin Islands,
Denmark, Sweden, Italy, and England. Some family.

And we were supposed to be its "typical" members.

As I thought about it, though, I realized that
the commercial didn't show Crawford City and its
people as typical at all. This was much better than
typical. It was much better than real.

Then the rest of the commercials began showing up on television—morning, noon, and night.
We were excited about seeing those ads, too, but
by the time they were shown on nationwide television, it was June, school was out, and my friends
and I had graduated. Also, by then we knew who
the stars of the other five commercials would be.

CHAPTER 2

Although everybody in school was excited about the Burg-O-Rama commercials and the possibility of being on national TV, during the month of March some other things happened that were even more exciting. March was basketball tournament time.

Crawford City is in the absolute heart of basketball country, sitting in the southern tip of Ohio and practically surrounded by West Virginia, Kentucky, and Indiana, all big basketball states. When the state high school tournament begins, basketball is just about all that anybody wants to talk about. MARCH MADNESS is what the local newspapers call it.

Crawford High basketball fans have not always had much to cheer about. In spite of all the interest around town, the school's sports history is not that brilliant. Sophomore year I was on the debate

team and we visited a high school in Akron that
had a trophy case stuffed with gold basketballs
and footballs and pictures of championship teams.
There has never been a trophy case like that at
Junius P. Crawford High School. In fact, the only
sign of athletic success you can find around town
is in the Stop 'N' Snack luncheonette across the
square from the school, an old-fashioned kind of
soda fountain that has the same light-green linoleum on the floors and the counters and the table-
tops. Some Crawford varsity letters are nailed on
the wall next to a faded picture of a hot fudge
sundae, and sitting on a shelf with the water
glasses is a dusty trophy, a Morgan County
League football championship from 1959. The
owner of the Stop 'N' Snack, Gus Buteris, had a
son on that team. The football team hasn't won a
championship since, and until lately the basketball teams haven't done any better.

Things started to change, though, when Jeff
Leuders began playing basketball for Crawford
four years ago. Jeff was six feet seven inches tall as
a freshman, and now he is six nine. He's a little
skinny, but he is tough, strong, and very quick. He
plays center, and the team is built around him.

A year ago they won the Morgan County
League and went all the way to the quarterfinal
round of the state tournament—the "Elite Eight"
—before losing a close game to a gigantic school
from Cleveland. This year everybody around here

figured the guys had a shot at the state champion-ship, and even the Cleveland *Free Press*, which probably had never heard of Crawford City until a year ago, picked us to finish second or third in the state.

Through the regular season nothing happened to disappoint anybody. The team went undefeated in the league, and even more important, around Christmastime they won a couple of games down in Cincinnati. All the sportswriters said that was the big test: playing against inner-city schools. But the reporters did something that I hate and will never do in my paper—they tried to slant the story. They made the games a racial mat-ter, because Crawford City is practically an all white town, and the teams from Cincinnati were mostly black. The question all the papers asked—or hinted at if they didn't say it directly—was whether a bunch of white country boys could beat those black city kids. As it turned out, we could, but it seems to me that the papers shouldn't have raised the question of skin color at all.

It's also too bad that when we won, the Cincin-nati sportswriters gave Jeff a nickname, "the White Tornado." I won't use that name in the *Tiger Eye*, and I sent a letter complaining to the editor of the Cincinnati *Herald*, but he didn't print it.

Anyway, our team made it to the Elite Eight again this year, and Jeff Leuders was averaging just under forty points a game. The quarterfinals would be played at the Civic Arena in Cincinnati, and once again all the papers had raised the White Tornado thing, because our opponent would be Cincinnati Roosevelt, an inner-city team that was ranked number two in the state.

I wanted to capture some of the excitement for my paper, but of course I couldn't get day-after coverage of the game into the *Tiger Eye*. So instead, I decided to do a pregame issue featuring interviews with the coach and some of the players and some kids-in-the-corridor. Of course, I wanted an interview with Jeff Leuders to be the big feature, and several days before the game I spoke to Dr. McCollom, who let Jeff and me out of sixth period—him from economics, me from trigonometry. I sort of picked up Jeff outside his classroom, and as we were walking down the hall, Kelly Flynn came along and gave me a sly wink and a questioning look as if something peculiar was going on.

"Let's get out of here," I said to Jeff. "We'll never be able to talk around school."

You're really not supposed to leave the school grounds without approval, but I figured that Dr. McCollom had given us approval enough, so we headed across the square to the Stop 'N' Snack. I'm sure we looked like Mutt and Jeff to anybody watching us. Jeff *was* Jeff, of course, all six nine of him, while I top out at five seven, not really short, but a dwarf next to him. Jeff slouched along beside me, leaning over as if to get down to my height. I'm sure people have been on him about his posture for years, but, like many tall people, he's self-conscious. The only time he stands up straight is when he plays basketball. I suppose that's when it counts.

Mr. Buteris gave Jeff a big hello as we went into the Stop 'N' Snack and nodded to me. I don't think he knows who I am, though I come in fairly often so he at least recognizes me. We both ordered something to drink, Jeff a glass of milk, me a Tab, and it was time to begin the interview.

Before the interview, back in the *Tiger Eye* office, I had written down some questions for Jeff and then more or less memorized them. I figure that interviews go better if I act like I'm having a conversation, not reading a list of prepared questions. Usually that strategy works for me, but this day—maybe it was the silence, or maybe it was that Jeff was really a big star around school and around the state—I suddenly got nervous and forgot my whole set of questions. This was really odd because Jeff and I were not exactly strangers. We'd gone to the same elementary school— Central—and were in the same eighth grade class. We had even worked on a project together, a model of the Pilgrims' Landing with a papier-mâché Plymouth Rock and a plastic model of the *Mayflower* that Jeff had put together from a kit.

I was desperate for a lead question. I hadn't

thought interviewing him would be this hard. "Do you like basketball?" I asked, nervous. And I laughed stupidly.

Actually, it was not such a stupid question. It was an echo of something I'd heard in elementary school:

"Jeff has got to *like* basketball if he's going to play it well."

That had been said by Mr. Edward Jackson, our eighth grade science teacher, who also coached the Central team.

"It's not up to me to decide if he likes it enough to want to play."

At that time Jeff was thirteen years old and a skyscraping six five.

"Because of his height," Mr. Jackson had said, "a lot of people will be after him to play, whether he wants to or not. I'll help him all I can, but only if he says he *likes* basketball."

Jeff certainly needed a lot of help in those days. He had grown so fast that he was badly coordinated, and I can remember feeling sorry for him. Though he was big, he couldn't move fast or jump very high. In the elementary league games he would stand near the basket and our players would lob passes to him, high above everybody's outstretched hands. When Jeff caught the ball—which he couldn't always do—he would turn to the basket and score two points while the little people all around pulled at his jersey. Central

School always won, but those games were dull. Obviously Jeff had told Mr. Jackson that, yes, he wanted to play basketball. They spent hours and hours together in the gym, working on foul shots, jump shots, tip-ins. So, in spite of asking what sounded like a dumb question, it was natural for me to ask if Jeff still enjoyed the game.

He laughed with me. "Yes, I like basketball."

"I only asked," I said, "because I remember what Mr. Jackson said in eighth grade."

He smiled. "I remember too. Mr. Jackson was a great coach. Probably the best coach I've ever had. I miss him."

Mr. Jackson had left Central a couple of years later, for California, I think. Quite a few kids from the high school would go back and visit him, and then suddenly he was gone. Somebody said he got a better job teaching in a junior college.

"Do you ever hear from him?" I asked.

"Not anymore. He wrote me a couple of times after he moved away. But then—you know—I never wrote back and he stopped."

"Yes, I know."

Jeff played with the wet ring his milk glass had left on the green linoleum tabletop. "The thing that was so good about Mr. Jackson is that he never pushed anybody. Never yelled at people or anything like that. He simply told you what you were doing good or bad and helped you work on it."

"Is it different at Crawford?"

He looked at me, sizing me up, it seemed.

"Yes," he said slowly, "it's different."

"How? Is it more competitive, or what?"

"Oh, much more competitive." He paused for a moment, thinking. "Don't get me wrong," he said finally. "Please. Coach Byram is really good. He's helped me a lot."

What was Jeff getting at? I didn't know, so I kept my mouth shut and nodded.

"But," he went on, "the high school coaches are more serious about it. More serious about winning."

"I suppose they recognize your talent. They probably know you've made the school a winner. You've made *them* winners. I guess they have a lot riding on you."

Jeff suddenly looked completely dejected and miserable. "I wish it wasn't so." He stopped talking.

"I'm sorry," I said. "Did I say something wrong?"

"No, no," Jeff answered, giving me a wave of his hand. "It's just that expression, 'riding on you.' I must have heard it a hundred times this year."

"Who besides me has used it?"

"Everybody. My parents. The coaches. The newspapers. Even people in the street stop me. 'Good luck,' they say. 'Our hopes are riding on you.'"

He paused, thinking.

"And?" I prodded him.

"And I don't see why it has to be that way. That's what I mean about the coaches being more serious."

"I'm sorry, I don't follow you."

"Well, you remember the elementary school days?"

I nodded.

"I was, let's face it, just a goon when I played. A big tall goon."

I nodded ever so slightly. What else could I do?

"I was the big center who scored all the points because I was bigger than everybody else."

I nodded again. Keep talking, Jeff.

"Well, in high school, I've developed. I can play all over the court, outside and inside, and I've got a good shot."

He sighed again and looked down into his empty milk glass. "But they're still using me as the goon. They keep me in the middle, close to the basket, and just tell me to take the short shots, the easy stuff."

"But that's what gets the points, isn't it?"

"Sure, but that's the problem."

I didn't understand, so I raised my eyebrows.

"Well, Coach Byram says I've *got* to be in the middle and I've *got* to get forty points every game. Everything's riding on it, he says."

"How could they do it any different?"

"There are five of us on that team," Jeff said, and I nodded, showing my great knowledge of basketball. "Maybe I'm a little better than the other guys, but they're good too. I'm not carrying them. I don't have to carry them. I don't *want* to carry them."

"To have them 'riding' on you?"

"Yes. Right. And I also think that I'd be a better player that way—playing all over, not just inside. I figure that when I get to college, I'm not going to be able to keep on being the goon."

"You're not the goon now, Jeff."

"You know what I mean, Karen. In college I won't be the biggest guy there. I'll probably play power forward, not center. I'll be a playmaker, not a high-scoring center. I want to do that now. But the coach says that we're winning, and we have to stick to our game plan."

"Wow," I said. "You're under a lot of pressure."

"Yeah. Like last week, they invited me to the Kiwanis club for lunch, you know?"

I didn't know, actually, but I wanted to follow this wherever Jeff wanted to take it.

"It was nice and all that, but I had the feeling that they already just assumed the state championship was won. 'Here's the White Tornado,' they said, 'who will make us number one.' I hate that expression, 'the White Tornado.'"

"Me too." I told him about my letter to the Cincinnati *Herald*.

"Thanks," he said, "but it won't do any good. You and I are the only ones who don't like it. Everybody else thinks it's terrific."

"You know how fans get," I suggested, trying to be reassuring. "A lot of what they do is just because they're proud. They want to get behind a winner."

He shook his head, looking both sad and angry, if that's possible. "But what if we lose? What if we go down to Cincinnati and get beat? Or if we make it to the finals in Columbus and then lose up there?"

I could see what he was worried about. Last year when the team lost in the quarterfinals, the local paper had been nasty about the way they'd played, even though nobody had expected them to get that far in the first place. Still, I tried to help Jeff be philosophical about it.

"A loss is a loss. It's no big deal. All that really matters is whether you played your best." I had heard that someplace, but I didn't quote it exactly, I know.

"*You* feel that way," he said, "and I do . . . sort of. But we're the only ones. Everybody else just cares if we win."

Jeff looked around the Stop 'N' Snack. Except for Mr. Buteris, who was washing some dishes, the place was empty. He lowered his voice. "You won't tell anybody something, will you?"

"No," I answered, "of course not. I can keep a secret."

"I just wish we could play the game now."

Was that his secret? That was no big deal.

"I mean," he continued, "that I just wish we could get together with the other team and play a pickup game without coaches or fans around. I know I should be grateful for all the support and all that, but I wish they would go away and leave me alone."

Now I thought I could see what had happened.

"Jeff," I said, "it seems to me that you're creating the pressure yourself, or at least some of it. I think the biggest thing riding on you is yourself." I suddenly had an image of Jeff riding on his own shoulders, pounding his head with his fists, and I laughed.

He didn't know what I was laughing at, but he smiled back.

"I know it sounds corny," I said, "and I'm just a friend, not a coach or anything, but I think you ought to stop carrying around whatever it is that you're carrying around. I believe you when you say you love basketball. I can see your eyes light up. I think you should just play the game and ignore what people think. You don't owe them anything. Relax and play *your* game. And *enjoy* it."

"Well, maybe," he said, but he was shaking his

head. As an adviser, I wasn't doing so hot, and somehow *I* felt as if something was riding on that.

"At least know this, Jeff," I said. "If you don't score forty points every game and don't win the state championship, I won't be disappointed. I won't ride on you."

He gave me a slow smile, unenthusiastic. "Yeah, thanks."

I saw some kids go past outside the Stop 'N' Snack, and a couple others came in. Sixth period, and the school day, had ended.

"We ought to go," I said. "You've probably got to practice. But before we leave, I want to ask one question."

"Okay."

"Forgetting about the Kiwanis Club and the fans and the coaches and the newspapers, do you think this team is good enough to win the state championship?"

He thought for a moment.

"Yes," he said, "I do."

And his eyes lit up.

I never wrote a story about Jeff Leuders for the *Tiger Eye*. I just didn't know what to say. I suppose I could have done a story with some sort of headline like BASKETBALL STAR PREDICTS VICTORY, which is what everybody wanted to hear. But that wouldn't have been a complete story; it would have been just as slanted as when the regular papers called Jeff the White Tornado and set him up against the black kids. I daydreamed about writing a story—the real story—with the headline, BASKETBALL STAR TELLS COACH, FANS, "GO AWAY." *That* would bring me some readers and turn the school on its ear. But that would also have been unfair to Jeff, spilling his secret, and I really didn't seriously consider doing it.

So still in quest of something to write, I went to a huge pep dance the Friday night before the game. I didn't have a date, and I felt a little foolish going without somebody. Playing girl reporter gave me an excuse, though, and besides, I would have felt more foolish staying home alone on a Friday night when everybody else was down at the school.

I once saw a joke in *Mad* magazine about a high school prom committee that rented an expensive hotel ballroom and then decorated it to look just like the high school gym where they usually had their dances. Our pep dance committee—with Kelly Flynn in charge, of course—had done their best to make the Crawford High gym look like something other than a gym by covering it from floor to ceiling with orange and black crepe paper, but they had simply made it into a high school gym that looked like it was ready for a Halloween dance. (I've never liked our school colors. Though our guys are supposed to be Tigers, kids from other schools call them the Hollow Weenies because of their orange and black suits.)

By the time I got there, the dance was in full swing, with music blaring out of the speakers and a mob of people out on the floor. I looked around and spotted my friends in their usual places. Kelly and Tom were over in the Senior Corner, the end of the gym that is by tradition the hangout for seniors, where underclassmen don't dare go. (I don't know what would happen if they did, but nobody has ever tried.) Kelly was in her cheerleading outfit—orange sweater, black skirt with orange pleats, white sneakers, and white socks with an orange stripe—and she was beaming up at Tom with her my-hero look. Jane Heath was nearby, talking with some senior girls, and if the evening went according to form, she would spend most of her time there, maybe dancing once or twice with other guys, but really waiting for Tom to ask her. It seemed hopeless to me, the way she waited for him.

George Foley was out in the middle of the dance floor with a cute girl, probably a sophomore he had decided to give a thrill. George always came to the dances alone, too, not because he couldn't get a date, but because he didn't want to be slowed down by being stuck with one woman.

Over in another corner I spotted the Burg-O-Rama cameraman, the Big Fella, with his bags of equipment. That guy was everyplace these days, always peering through the viewfinder as if that was actually his eyes. The light seemed pretty dim in the gym for pictures, but he was swinging his camera back and forth at the crowd.

The music stopped and some guy came on the microphone, talking a mile a minute, pretending to be a disc jockey. Most of what he said I couldn't understand, but I caught that the next dance was ladies' choice. Right away Jane asked Tom, and Kelly headed off to find somebody to dance with, probably the next handsomest senior jock. I decided to give George Foley a thrill of his own and walked over. He was not too happy to see me coming, and the sophomore girl, who probably wanted to ask him to dance but was afraid, gave me a dirty look.

"Hi, George," I said. "Ladies' choice, and you're mine."

"Oh, hello, Karen," he said in a voice that sounded like he'd just flunked his trigonometry examination. He turned to the girl and smiled. "I'll catch up with you later, okay?" She looked at him as if she'd just been hit by Cupid's arrow and smiled back shyly.

"Yeah," I said to her, "I won't wear him out for you."

I suppose I shouldn't have been nasty to her, but George sometimes makes me mad, and he's sure not all that helpful to my ego. I turned and walked out on the dance floor, letting him follow.

As soon as the music started, though, I was sorry I'd asked him. It was a fast number, and I'm only good at the slow ones. George is a good dancer in his own way. He's relaxed and loose and kind of funny—arms flying, hips swaying, unembarrassed to be out in the center of things—and I'm just the opposite, feeling as if everybody is watching my mistakes. But actually, everybody— or at least the younger female set—was watching George, who managed to eyeball every girl within twenty feet as he flailed away, looking right past me to check out his possibilities for the rest of the night. So as we swirled and whirled, I looked around a bit myself, and I spotted Jeff Leuders, who was out on the floor, too, easy to spot, because he was a head taller than everybody else there.

Everybody, that is, except Marianne Lucas, the girl who had asked him to dance. She's at least six two or six three herself, a basketball player and captain of the girls' volleyball team. She's not an especially attractive girl, and her height probably causes her some problems, but she does okay, and if being tall bothers her, she doesn't let it show. In fact, she's a good dancer, and with her long arms and legs, she was putting on a real show. Jeff, on the other hand, seemed miserable, as if he looked silly, which, I would have to admit, he did. He was staring straight ahead grimly. More than anything, he reminded me of that gawky eighth grade basketball player I had felt sorry for.

George was paying enough attention to me to

follow my gaze—maybe he thought I was seeing something he'd missed—and said something, nodding toward Jeff and Marianne.

"What?" I yelled, to be heard over the music.

He motioned across the floor. "String Bean and Spaghetti! What a pair."

"You shouldn't call them that," I shouted back. "They can't help it."

"No harm meant," he yelled cheerfully, spinning away from me.

"But maybe harm done," I shouted back as he turned toward me again.

He dipped at the knees and leaned back, holding up his hands as if to defend himself.

"Okay, Mom," he said. "Okay." And he spun and danced alone for a bit, his back to me.

Well, I was sorry to act like an old lady, but knowing how Jeff felt, I didn't think he needed that sort of stuff, even if he couldn't hear what George had said. So George and I danced in the silence of all that uproar, not saying anything more until the music stopped. Then he turned and gave me an elaborate bow.

"Thank you, ma'am," he said. "It was a pleasure."

Liar.

"The pleasure was all mine," I lied back, returning his bow, and we headed in the direction of the Senior Corner.

I could tell that George was mad at me, so I

thought I'd see if I could get back in tune with him.

"Look," I said, "I didn't mean to be a busybody or anything, but I figure that Jeff and Marianne have enough troubles with their height. We don't need to make fun of them."

"Trouble?" George said. "Old Jeffrey is going to make a fortune with that string bean height of his. He's going to play college ball for about two years, then turn pro and sign a contract for a million bucks." He grinned at me. "And you can print that—it's a Foley exclusive prophecy."

"Really? I mean, a million dollars? For sure? That soon?"

"You can bet on it," George said, and if George said he would bet on anything, you knew he was dead serious. "Jeff will be a millionaire before he's twenty-one."

"Incredible," I said. "Incredible."

George nodded in agreement.

Then, curious, I asked, "What do you know about Jeff? You've probably played ball with him. What's he like?"

George raised an eyebrow. "What's this? You interested in him? You want to marry a millionaire? I can fix you up if you want."

"No!" I said loudly. Too loudly. Just because I didn't think Jeff was a freak didn't mean I wanted to go out with him. "I mean, I'm just curious to know what he's like away from school, away from sports."

"I hardly know," George said with a shrug. "I don't think anybody knows, at least not any of the guys I hang around with. He never spends any time with us varsity ath-uh-letes. He sticks to himself."

"Who does?" asked Jane Heath, walking up, her arm linked through Tom's.

"Jeff Leuders," George answered.

"Do you know him, Tom?" I asked. "Very well, I mean?"

"Not all that well," he replied. "I just know that he's got it made as a basketball player. He's just all set."

"That's what George told me. Do you think Jeff will go pro in a couple of years?"

"Probably," Tom said, and suddenly he looked sad, and his whole body seemed to sag a little bit. "Lucky stiff."

I knew that Tom had once dreamed of going to college on a football scholarship, but with the football team's bad year—winning only three games—nobody had recruited him. Tom was a good athlete, but just plain not good enough to do much after high school. Still, his reaction toward Jeff surprised me a bit, because Tom was generally a good-natured kid and never seemed jealous of anybody.

"Well, what the heck," I said. "It's great that somebody from this town will make it big, eh?"

Tom was about to say something else, something nasty, from the look on his face, but the music started, a slow dance. I think he was going to ask Jane to dance, but Kelly suddenly showed up and placed her hand through Tom's other arm, telling us—and especially Jane—that he was hers.

"Hello, Karen," she said, seeing me for the first time. "Having a big night?"

There was no edge on her voice or anything, but she got in her dig and I was lost for a quick reply.

"Hello, Kelly," I said. "Big enough." A dumb thing to say.

Kelly tugged gently at Tom's arm, wanting him to dance, and Jane obliged by sliding her hand out. Then, just as Kelly and Tom were starting out on the dance floor, something caught the Power Mongers' eyes and they all four looked past me onto the dance floor. Actually, they seemed to be looking *above* me.

There was a tap on my shoulder. I turned and had to look up myself. It was Jeff Leuders.

"Would you like to dance?" he said quietly, looking down at me but also over at the Mongers as if to see whether or not they would approve.

I was stunned, but I kept myself together. "Sure," I said, all eloquence. I turned with him and quickly walked out toward the center of the floor to get out of the range of the Power Mongers. As I left, though, I could see that their eyes were wide.

The music was slow, my kind of dance music, but that was the most awkward dance I'd ever had in my life. In the first place, you'd be amazed at the difference fourteen inches in height makes. Like, if you look at a ruler, it's only two inches more than that, but when fourteen inches is how much taller the guy is, it's amazing. The top of my head only came to the second button on his shirt, and my eyes were even with the third button. When I looked up at him, his face seemed about three feet away, and I had to shout up at him.

"How's it going?" I hollered to make conversation.

"Okay," he said softly, so I could hardly hear him, and he didn't say anything else. We were both embarrassed, and I was thinking he was probably sorry he asked me to dance. Somebody bumped into us, so we didn't try to continue the conversation, for which I was grateful. I felt terrifically self-conscious, because as we moved around, I could see the Power Mongers off in the distance watching us.

"Thanks," I said when the music stopped.

"Sure," he answered, and we stood there awkwardly.

"Well, good luck with the game," I finally said. "I know everything will be okay."

"Yeah," he said. "Well, thanks." And he left me there in the middle of the dance floor.

I didn't want to go back to the Senior Corner, but I couldn't avoid the Power Mongers either. So I walked back over.

"Going up in the world, eh, Wexler?" asked George, smirking. "I offered to introduce her to String Bean," he explained to the Mongers, "but she's got her own connections."

"My, my," said Kelly. "Who would have thought of such a thing?"

Tom didn't say anything, and neither did Jane, though she gave me a look that said, "Later. Let's talk about this later."

Actually there was nothing to tell. Jeff asking me to dance was as much of a mystery to me as it was to them.

George started to make some sort of joke about elevator shoes, and I was getting ready to tell him off, but before I could, the lights came on full, catching a few kids making out in the corners and causing everybody to blink. The pep band had set up near the DJ's stand and started playing the Crawford fight song. Kelly trotted away from us, and cheerleaders appeared from all over the gym, starting into their fight song routine as they ran. Coach Byram appeared from someplace, and when the song was over, he called for all the basketball players to come front and center, while the kids cheered. The Big Fella moved out of his cor-

ner, and I could see him filming away like mad,
catching the players, the band, the crowd.

The speech that Mr. Byram made was rah rah
and kind of corny, but most of the people cheered
every time he stopped to breathe. Then the team
starters muttered a few words in the microphone,
telling us all that, for sure, Crawford was the next
state champion. Jeff was the last one to speak and
he did the same thing, mumbling, but there was so
much cheering for him that you couldn't have
heard him even if he'd spoken clearly.

As I watched him standing by the microphone,
almost squirming with being uncomfortable, I
think I figured out why he had asked me to dance.
He wasn't interested in dating me or anything like
that. He was just a lonely guy, a guy who was
always the center of the show, but lonely just the
same. I felt sorry and awful for him. Maybe he
would make a million bucks before he was twenty-
one. But would it be worth it?

The Civic Arena in Cincinnati is just huge, so
big it's almost frightening. The place is a giant
dome, with everything made out of cement and
bright colored plastic. It was designed for all
kinds of sports—hockey, basketball, indoor soccer
—and they even hold rodeos and the circus there.
The program said it seats twenty-five thousand for
basketball games, and the night of the quarterfinals it was packed.

I went alone, taking the pep bus down (if you can call being on a bus with fifty-four other kids "alone"). We were one of eight buses in a caravan from Crawford City. Some people from the town drove down separately, and the two thousand seats that had been allotted to Crawford City were all filled.

We arrived midway through the first quarter-final game between Dayton North and Lancaster Senior High, and the place was already bedlam. I can't remember the score, but it was close, and fans from both sides were screaming at the players and at each other. The bands from those schools were set up at opposite ends of the arena, and both were playing at once, even when the game was going on.

My seat was a long way up, probably fifty or sixty rows, but fairly close to midcourt. The players below looked small, and the glare of the lights made it seem as if you were watching the game on color TV. I thought about Jeff Leuders and looked around this huge place and literally felt sick.

We took our seats, and right away the pep club leaders started passing out orange and black pennants and pompons. Everybody started cheering, first at random, then in unison:

"Crawford. . . . Crawford. . . . Crawford."

When the kids from Cincinnati Roosevelt—the "Big Reds," our opponents—saw us, they broke out red and white streamers and pennants and chanted back:

"Go Red. . . . Go White. . . . Go Roosevelt."

Our band unpacked and began warming up. So did theirs. Our band played our fight song. Theirs played theirs. The other two schools and their bands were still going at it. Nobody was watching the game.

And for a while I had one of those feelings of total unreality, as if I didn't know where I was, as if I was somehow apart from the whole scene. As a reporter, I always try to be detached, an objective observer, but this feeling was more than that. I sat there taking it all in, wondering why everybody was here, why people were so excited. Eventually, though, I got myself back to reality, and when our cheerleaders, led by Kelly, showed up on the floor and took their seats in the first row, I started yelling with everybody else. We were even cheering the cheerleaders.

Somebody finally won the first game and the winners and losers left. Immediately the Roosevelt cheerleaders took the floor and did some sort of dance number with their band. Next our kids started a cheer that, at least from my point of view, was a lot more interesting than theirs.

Then at one end of the arena, at the end of a dark tunnel that led somewhere under the seats, I saw Jeff Leuders. It was too far away for me to see his expression, but he was standing there casually, looking around, holding a basketball on his hip and seeming a lot more relaxed than I would have been in his situation. The rest of the team was lined up behind him, and as soon as Kelly and the girls finished their cheer, Jeff led the team out. The Crawford crowd screamed, and the cheerleaders did little solo exercises on the sidelines: handstands, cartwheels, jumps, and splits.

Jeff ran with a long, relaxed lope, his warm-up trousers, which had kind of bell bottoms, flapping loosely. He dribbled through the center circle and headed for the Crawford basket, picking up speed. He took off just past the foul line and jumped so high his elbows were even with the rim of the basket. You're not allowed to dunk the ball during warm-up, so instead of cramming it down through the net in a slam dunk, Jeff flipped it up softly, and it dropped cleanly through the net. Classy. The crowd roared and the Tigers went into a razzle-dazzle lay-up drill.

The Roosevelt Big Reds came on from the other end and their fans cut loose. Roosevelt's team looked smaller than ours, and man for man we would have a height advantage. But they also seemed quick, and I watched some of them shoot from the outside—they were deadly. A few players from both sides lined up at center court to watch the other team warm up, but not Jeff. He just took his shots, popping them in from long and short range, paying no attention to the opposition.

Good for him, I thought. He looked great. Relaxed and in control. If he was nervous, he didn't show it.

The buzzer sounded to end the warm-up, and the bands battled it out for a minute, both playing, everybody on both sides singing and shouting. We sent out our usual starting five, with Jeff jumping center. Roosevelt started four black kids, all of them lanky and looking quick, and, surprisingly, a white kid who didn't even *look* like a basketball player. This guy was actually chubby, though he had huge muscular arms and legs and looked like a wrestler. Even more surprising, this bruiser lined up opposite Jeff at center. He was at least four inches shorter than Jeff, and there was no way he could win the tip-off. Everybody in the stands started talking about him.

The referee tossed the ball up and Jeff skyed, outjumping the kid by about four feet and tapping the ball easily to one of our forwards, who dribbled downcourt and flipped it back to Jeff at the foul circle. Jeff drove the lane and went up for a jumper, a clear and simple shot from about six feet out, one of his favorites.

And then the Bruiser hit him. Not with his fists, I mean, but with that big body. Jeff missed his shot and a foul was called. He hit both free throws, and we took a 2–0 lead. The Crawford fans were happy and showed it.

We quickly learned what Roosevelt's strategy was going to be. The Bruiser didn't come to shoot baskets. He didn't really come to play basketball. It was his job to lean on Jeff, because whenever Jeff got the ball, the guy would muscle into him, pushing and shoving. Sometimes a foul was called, but often the Bruiser did it when the ref was looking someplace else, so he wouldn't get caught. In the stands we were all screaming, trying to tell the ref about it.

When Roosevelt went on offense, the Bruiser didn't even look for the ball, and nobody passed it to him. He looked for Jeff and pushed him away from the basket so he couldn't play defense or rebound. It was shabby, and I joined in booing the Bruiser, even though I think booing is bad sportsmanship.

The strategy was paying off, though. The only points Jeff was getting were at the foul line, and he wasn't getting all that many. At the other end of the court, with Jeff tangled up, the Roosevelt sharpshooters were pouring in points. They opened up a small lead, and then larger. Our guys were playing like they were stuck in mud. With Jeff out of commission, the other four didn't seem to know what to do.

Then our fans started to get on Jeff.

"What's the matter with Leuders?" some loudmouth guy—a Crawford fan—yelled behind me. "He's not doing a thing out there."

Couldn't he see that Jeff was being manhandled?

"He just doesn't have it tonight," somebody else complained. "He just doesn't have what it takes to play against these city kids."

Down on the court Jeff was working like a horse. I could see that he was tense. His long, easy stride had tightened up, and he was stooping as he ran, not standing up straight. Somebody passed him the ball outside the foul ring, and before the Bruiser could catch up with him, Jeff fired off a jumper, too long, that missed the rim and went out of bounds.

"Air ball!" screamed the man behind me. "That was no shot. What's the *matter* with him?"

I turned around and gave the guy a dirty look, but he didn't pay attention to me.

Roosevelt took the ball out of bounds and brought it downcourt quickly. A sharpshooter let one go from outside and it bounded high off the rim. The Bruiser muscled in front of Jeff and a small Roosevelt kid slipped by, snagged the rebound, and popped in a quick two points.

"C'mon, Leuders," screamed the man. "Get the lead out. Rebound, for crying out loud."

And so it went. By the end of the first half, Roosevelt had a twelve-point lead. Jeff had just nine points, five of them on foul shots, and only two baskets from the floor. The Crawford crowd had grown silent, all except the loudmouth behind me, who was telling his wife they ought to go home now.

I knew what was happening down there. It was not just that the Bruiser was playing football instead of basketball. I could see the strain on Jeff's face as he left the court, and it was the same look he'd given me at the Stop 'N' Snack when he was talking about the pressure he felt. Jeff was trying to carry the whole team, trying to do everything. People had said everything was riding on him, and he had picked up the burden and was trying to carry it alone.

"It's not worth it, Jeff," I shouted, but of course he couldn't hear me. "Let the others do it." I don't believe in telepathy and all that, but I hoped my thoughts would reach him.

During the halftime the Roosevelt people dominated the show. They cheered almost nonstop, and their band played tune after tune. Kelly got our girls out for a couple of cheers, but they had no enthusiasm. I turned around and looked at the Crawford crowd. They were stone-faced. A bunch of bad losers, I thought, and I knew what my next editorial for the *Tiger Eye* would be about.

As I looked around the arena, I spotted the Burg-O-Rama Man near one of the baskets. He was all dressed up in a suit as usual, and beside him was the Big Fella in jeans and a sport shirt, filming away, his camera pointed at the cheerleaders. Kelly spotted them, too, and she gave a big smiling wave. When she sat down, she

checked her hair in her compact mirror and fluffed
it up. She was more interested in looking good on
film than helping out the team. I wished I had a
photograph of that to use with my editorial,
which I thought maybe I'd call BAD LOSERS. Just
for the heck of it, I stood up and yelled, waving
my arms, begging the Crawford people: "C'mon
everybody. Don't quit now. Let's stick with them.
Let's hear some noise."

The only noise I heard was the Roosevelt
crowd, "Go Red. Go White." I felt like a fool and I
embarrassed the pep club girls around me. Nobody else stood up, so I sat down.

The teams came back on the floor and warmed
up again. The Roosevelt kids were loose and looking sharp. Our guys were down, listless, and the
game seemed as good as over.

The second half began just like the first, only
going in the other direction. Jeff easily won the
center jump from the Bruiser, tapping the ball to a
forward and taking a return pass at the foul circle.
He drove into the lane and pulled up for a shot,
just like in the first half, and the Bruiser came
charging over to hit him. Then, suddenly, without
even looking, Jeff fired off a pass to one of our
forwards who was all alone under the basket for
an easy two points.

"Hey hey," somebody in the crowd yelled.
"Nice!"

Roosevelt brought down the ball and a guard passed it to a sharpshooter, who went up for a fifteen-footer. But Jeff came charging out from nowhere, skyed, and blocked the shot. One of our guards scooped up the ball and started a fast break. The Bruiser was left standing alone under the basket, looking for somebody to hit. The closest person was a Roosevelt cheerleader standing on the sidelines, and he passed her up.

Things had changed. Jeff was running loose, chattering with the guys around him. The Crawford crowd knew it was different and came back alive. Turncoats. I was really angry with them and added another mental paragraph to my editorial.

During that second half Jeff hardly shot at all, but he kept the Bruiser busy and made sharp, clever passes, setting up other people for easy baskets. On defense he was all over the place blocking shots, while the Bruiser ran after him, trying to keep up. In the meantime, the other four Crawford guys were cleaning up on rebounds and running fast breaks.

"The kids are taking up the slack," said the loudmouth behind me. "Leuders can't handle it, so the rest of them are carrying the load. Great bunch of kids."

Carrying the load! He didn't even know what was going on. I was sorry he hadn't left at half-time.

We whittled away at the lead and eventually went ahead, first by two points, then five, then eight. Halfway through the fourth period, the Bruiser fouled out. We booed him again. The guy was absolutely exhausted and sat on the bench, his head covered with a towel, breathing in great gasps.

His substitute was a taller kid, almost Jeff's height, who looked like a basketball player instead of a wrestler. But the first time Jeff got the ball, he looked the new kid in the eye, paused, and cocked his arm to shoot. The kid jumped to block the shot and Jeff drove around him, dribbling the ball just once, taking two giant strides down the foul lane, and doing a stuff shot that shook the entire backboard.

That did it for me. I started to cry.

"What's the matter?" said a pep club girl next to me.

"Contact lens," I lied.

I was just happy for Jeff.

And, I guess, happy for us, too, for about that time we all knew that Crawford City was going to win the basketball championship of the state of Ohio, and I knew that I would never have to write my editorial on BAD LOSERS.

I didn't see what happened in the locker room after the Roosevelt game. Crawford City is not sophisticated enough to let female reporters into the men's locker room, so I had to rely on hearsay. But I'm told that the guys were celebrating, really happy to have won after coming back from so far down. Then suddenly they became aware of the Burg-O-Rama Man standing there. The Big Fella was right beside him with his camera.

The Burg-O-Rama Man put his arm around Jeff, but not too tight, not tight enough to get his suit sweaty, and said, "Congratulations, Jeff. Fine game. When we get back to Crawford City, I'd like to take you to lunch."

◆　◆　◆

OPENING SHOT: A hand, slender, fingers stretched wide.

MUSIC: A single chord, first soft, then growing louder.

SHOT: The camera pulls back slowly, showing that the hand is holding a basketball. Arms show— lean arms, but well-muscled—tensed. The face appears: Jeff Leuders staring at something off camera.

MUSIC: Breaks into the Burg-O-Rama fight song motif.

SHOT: Now motion, a swirl of basketball players. Camera pulls back to show Jeff facing the Roosevelt substitute center.

ANNOUNCER: Burg-O-Rama would like you to meet Jeff Leuders of Crawford High School.

SHOT: Jeff makes his move, faking the opponent

and driving for the basket. The camera retreats as he drives in.

ANNOUNCER: In Ohio, they call him the Crawford City Tornado.

SHOT: Jeff leaps, stuffs the ball into the basket. The camera peers up at him through the net. Freeze: Jeff's face a mixture of determination and joy.

ANNOUNCER: And he led Crawford High School to the championship of the state of Ohio.

SHOTS: Crowd scenes. Cheerleaders leaping and hugging. Fans mobbing the team. Players laughing in the locker room. Jeff's face above the crowd, smiling, a basketball net hanging around his neck.

ANNOUNCER: Jeff spends every spare moment on the basketball court.

SHOT: Jeff on the high school playground, practicing his jump shot.

ANNOUNCER: But if you can't find him there, you might just find him at the nearest Burg-O-Rama.

SHOT: Jeff in a Burg-O-Rama booth holding onto a hamburger. The camera zooms in on his hands, fingers spread, holding the burger. Jeff holds it up to his mouth, and just as he starts to take a bite, he looks at the camera out of the corner of his eye. Freeze.

SHOT: Burg-O-Rama logo fills the screen, then shrinks to upper-left corner. Announcement appears:

A promotional fee has been paid to the Crawford City, Ohio, Public Schools and to Jeffrey Leuders by the Burg-O-Rama Foundation, a division of Trimble Enterprises, Inc.

◆ ◆ ◆

Most kids around school were pleased that Jeff had been chosen for the commercial. He did, after all, bring us the state championship, and now there's a trophy case at Crawford with two huge trophies: one for the championship, and one for Jeff, who was the Most Valuable Player for the whole tournament. So people thought he deserved whatever he got.

There were a few complaints, though. Like at lunch, George suddenly started to get nasty.

"I told you we should have set up a pool for those commercials," he said, stuffing a sandwich into his mouth at the same time. "Jeff Leuders is the last person in this school who needs the money. You know some college is going to give him a full scholarship. And then there's all that money for playing pro ball. What's he need the Burg-O-Rama money for?"

In a way George had a point. Jeff *didn't* need the money. As it turned out, twenty or thirty big-time schools recruited him that spring, and finally the University of Kentucky gave him a four-year scholarship, all expenses paid. I think they would have given him a pet racehorse if he wanted one.

I was just about to say to the group that money was not really the point, when Tom Garver exploded.

"Money is not the point!" he shouted. "The point is that he's just not that good."

"What?" I said. "Are you kidding? Not that good?"

"Leuders is a freak," Tom continued. "That's all. Just a big freak."

Kelly, sitting next to Tom, nodded in agreement.

"No way," I replied. "No way. He's a terrific athlete."

I looked to Jane Heath for support, but she was just looking at Tom and not saying anything.

"No way yourself, Karen," George said. "Tom's right. Chop six inches off Leuders and you've got an ordinary ballplayer."

"But he *is* that tall," I argued, "and he's done great for that height. There are lots of tall guys around the state of Ohio, but *Jeff* is the Most Valuable."

Tom ignored me and kept talking to George. "And if he's such a great athlete, why didn't he play football?" Nobody answered, though Kelly, as usual, was nodding with Tom, even if she didn't know the answer.

"It's because he'd get killed out there," Tom

said. "That skinny freak would get broken in half. He's not an athlete." He picked up a paper up and crushed it.

Tom was getting angrier and angrier, but so was I. In fact, I was just about to say something, but Jane tapped her hand on my knee under the table to quiet me.

"It's okay, Tom," she said. "I think maybe you're right that Jeff would not be a good football player, but we should face it, on the basketball court he is very talented. We can't take that away from him."

Jane is a lot cooler under fire than I am, but she didn't do any good.

"He's just a freak," Tom said over again. "And I don't care what anybody says, there are guys around here who are better athletes. He didn't deserve it."

Tom got up and stormed off, not bothering to take his trash to the bin. Jane got up right away and caught up with him near the door, talking to him as they went out. Kelly and George looked at me and then followed them out, both looking puzzled.

I sat by myself, puzzled, too, because it just wasn't like Tom to blow up that way. He was a relaxed, fun-loving kind of guy, never mean, or at least not usually mean, and I couldn't figure out what was eating him. I know he felt he was as good an athlete as Jeff, but I couldn't believe that just being jealous of Jeff was enough to start this whole thing.

I was disappointed with Tom, too, not just angry, because I thought that Jeff *did* deserve to be rewarded and noticed. Not for bringing Crawford a state championship—though that was a great honor for the school—but because he got his head clear and became the kind of basketball player he really wanted to be. I'm not certain that Tom could even understand why Jeff was deserving and was a real winner.

My only other disappointment was that the Burg-O-Rama ad showed Jeff as a kind of showboat: the Crawford City Tornado. I was thankful that they didn't call him the *White* Tornado, but the real Jeff, the one I got to know just briefly, is a different person altogether.

CHAPTER 3

There wasn't much disagreement among the students at Crawford High School that Mr. Robert Walton was the best teacher in the school. He taught general science, chemistry, and biology, so almost everybody in the school had him at least once. I took his general science course as a freshman, and this year I was in his third period biology class along with the Power Mongers and some other friends. That class was the high point of our day—or, at least, of my school day.

Mr. Walton was at an age that's difficult to guess. He was definitely one of the younger teachers, but not as young as the new ones. I suppose he was in his late twenties or early thirties, but once they reach twenty-five or so, I can never tell what age they are.

The thing I liked about Mr. Walton was that you could talk about anything you wanted to in his classes, but it wasn't just baloney. He was a very efficient teacher and expected you to do the readings and the assignments on your own. At the beginning of each period he would review the text materials for about ten or fifteen minutes. Then, if there weren't any questions, he would open things up for discussion related to science, even if it didn't have much to do with biology.

Once we spent almost two weeks talking about automobile engines, because most of us, the boys as well as the girls, didn't really know anything about them and he figured we ought to. Mr. Walton explained how motors worked and about fuel consumption, and he ran off copies of a repair manual for us so that if our cars wouldn't start or overheated, we could check out what was wrong. He even took the whole class out into the faculty parking lot to work on his car. He put on a set of old coveralls over his school clothes and actually crawled underneath the car to show us how to change the oil. His car was maybe eight or ten years old and had almost a hundred thousand miles on it, but it was really in good shape, so you could tell he knew what he was doing.

Another time we got talking about birth control and had some frank discussions about it, going into more detail than the sex education class we'd taken as sophomores. Many of the kids just wanted to talk about love and sex, but Mr. Walton also took the discussion into population control and world hunger and problems like that. He helped us see that these were important issues, too, so we weren't just discussing whether or not high school kids should have sex. Somebody tried to trick him into talking about his own sex life, but he just brushed the question aside and went on.

We knew that he *had* a sex life because several afternoons each week two little kids, probably three and five years old, would meet him after school, along with his wife driving that old car. She was a pretty, slightly overweight brunette, and very friendly. She didn't know everybody's name, but she would give students a nice hello. Mr. Walton was the only one of the teachers who ever had his family around school, even if it was just to pick him up, and I think that's another reason people liked him. We had an idea of him as a person and a family man, not just a teacher.

You can imagine that it didn't take long after the Burg-O-Rama Man hit town for the topic to come up in Mr. Walton's class.

"I suppose," he said one morning after we had finished a lesson on tree bark—cambium, xylem, phloem, and all that—"I suppose you people have caught Burg-O-Rama fever along with everyone else around school. Are you counting your money already?"

"Well, not counting," said Kathy Scheffler, a junior.

"But it sure seems nice to think about," Kelly Flynn added.

"Are you all so enthusiastic about this Burg-O-Rama enterprise?" he asked.

"Not me," answered George Foley, who still thought the wealth ought to be pooled and said so.

"Ah, I see," replied Mr. Walton. "You don't like the distribution of wealth, George, but you have no scruples about participating in the project?"

"Scruples?"

"*Scruples*—doubts, reservations. Have you no doubts about the wisdom of seeing young people, your peers and you, drawn into the web of commercialism in America? Into being mere pawns in the chess game of fast-food franchising?"

Mr. Walton spoke like that and taught like that. He asked questions all the time, sometimes in language that was difficult to understand. He would keep on asking questions until he got what he wanted from you or until you understood the idea. He ended every question with a little smile, and I could never tell if he was amused by what he thought you might say or just looking forward to hearing it.

"I don't see anything wrong with it," George answered.

"Does anyone else?"

Nobody wanted to say anything. Often there

were long silences in Mr. Walton's class as he waited patiently for someone to talk.

I decided to break the silence.

"I know that at least one parent wrote to the *Sentinel* saying that we shouldn't be involved in selling junk food."

"That's interesting, Karen," he said, smiling at me, "but I would be more interested in knowing what *you* think. What *do* you think?"

"Ah . . . well," I said a little weakly, "I don't know exactly what to think. I remember that when the Burg-O-Rama Man answered that letter, he said that their hamburgers were *not* junk food. I think he said they were '100% natural.' "

"One hundred percent?" Mr. Walton asked, shooting his eyebrows up in surprise. " 'Natural,' did you say?"

I nodded.

" 'Natural.' " He stroked his chin and looked up at the light fixture. "Now what do you suppose that word means?"

"I suppose," I said, "that it means 'pure' and 'healthy.' Not artificial or anything like that."

"I suppose that's what one might assume," he said, nodding slowly, "or what *he*, Mr. Leseney, your 'Burg-O-Rama Man,' might *want* you to assume."

He paused, looking out the window. Then he turned and pointed a finger at me.

"Is dog-do healthy, Karen Wexler?"

He surprised me, and I blushed. People around me laughed quietly.

"No, of course not," I protested.

"Of course not," he said, echoing me. "But let me ask you this. Do you consider dog-do 'natural'? 'Not artificial or anything like that'?"

"Well," I answered slowly, stalling for time, trying to figure out what he was up to. "I guess you could say that it is."

"In what sense?" he asked. "Didn't you just tell me that 'natural' things were 'pure' and 'healthy'?" He gave me a big grin.

"I was talking about *hamburgers,* not dog droppings," I said. "There's a difference."

"Of course there is," he beamed. "You were using the word in a different context. Dog-do is certainly natural, but even a person like George who has no scruples would probably not claim that dog-do is pure and healthy. Would you, George?"

George simply waved him off and laughed. He had been had. Just like I had been had.

But there was more.

"What about dynamite, Karen?" Mr. Walton asked.

"What about it?"

"What about that marvelous invention of Alfred Nobel, used so skillfully by construction workers and saboteurs. Would you put dynamite on your list of natural products?"

"No, of course not."

"Well let me tell you, then, that dynamite is 100% natural, made from chemicals and minerals dug from the bosom of Mother Earth, wrapped in paper made from her own trees."

"But it's *manufactured*," said Doug Ellis, a senior. He had taken me off the hook and I glanced over in appreciation. "You just said Nobel *invented* it. That means it's not natural. It's man-made."

"Granted, Doug," Mr. Walton answered. "But the *ingredients* are natural. Through the wonders of chemistry, the *natural* raw materials are converted into ammonium nitrate—alias dynamite. But you could still say that it's '100% natural,' couldn't you?"

"If you could say that," George put in, "you could claim that just about anything is natural. I mean, everything comes from the earth in one way or another."

Mr. Walton smiled at him and winked. "Good point, George. And I suppose that your Burg-O-Rama Man could claim his food was '100% natural,' no matter what it contained." He walked to the window and looked out, letting us think.

That was typical Walton teaching. He'd lead you through a series of questions just like a trial lawyer, and before you knew it, you were saying something you didn't know you knew. Some of the kids told him he would have been good on the old

Perry Mason show, leading the innocent to freedom, trapping the guilty in the answers to their own questions.

Actually, we knew that Mr. Walton *was* interested in the law in a serious way. Once we'd seen a fat book on his desk, *Principles of Criminal Law.*

"What's that for?" Kelly had asked, always nosy.

"It's for a course I'm taking."

"A course," she said. "What kind?"

"A course in criminal justice. I'm taking it at the Cincinnati Legal Institute."

"Why?" George Foley had asked. "Are you thinking about becoming a criminal?"

"No," answered Mr. Walton, "because I'm considering becoming an attorney."

"What!" shouted Dianne Leighton, a pretty junior girl who had sort of a crush on Walton. "And leave teaching?"

"Why?" Kelly asked. "Don't you like us anymore?"

Mr. Walton looked at us seriously, one of the few times I'd seen him without at least the hint of a smile.

"No, Kelly. I like you people as much as ever. It doesn't make me happy to think about leaving teaching."

"Then why are you thinking about it?" Jane Heath had asked.

Mr. Walton gave us a small smile and answered her question with a question.

"Do you know how much money a high school teacher makes?"

Nobody really did, and Mr. Walton didn't tell us, exactly.

"It's not a lot," he explained. "But you know about inflation and the cost of living, though, don't you?"

That we knew. We had talked about it in class a month earlier, about what it was doing to people.

"That's two plus two, my friends. Can you imagine trying to raise a family on what a teacher makes?"

I had trouble imagining raising a family at all, but I knew what he meant.

"But couldn't you get a higher paying job around school?" Jane suggested. "Somebody told me that Dr. McCollom was a teacher before he moved up to principal."

"That sort of thing is a possibility," Mr. Walton answered, "one that my wife and I talked about at length. But I don't think I'd be content as a school administrator. Believe it or not, I like working with you people. I need a career where I can work directly with people all the time. Law seems to be a good place for that."

"How soon are you leaving?" Dianne Leighton asked, upset, close to tears. "Are you going to finish the term?"

He laughed and walked by Dianne, patting her on the shoulder.

"Oh, I'm not leaving right away," he said, "if ever. It would be years before I could finish a degree. When all you can do is take courses nights, it takes a long time to become a lawyer."

Dianne looked happier.

"In the meantime," Mr. Walton had continued, "I'll hone my lawyer skills on you people, trying to get you to think critically about what you're doing and saying."

"I should think," our teacher-lawyer said, facing the chalkboard, not the class, "that young people about to make fabulous sums of money selling something would want to know just how 'natural,' 'pure,' and 'healthy' the product was." He turned and pointed to us as if we were the jury. "Do you?"

We did.

And that's how our junk food unit—or more accurately, our unit on Nutrition and Processed Foods—got started. We each picked something about junk foods as a topic and worked up a report for the class.

My topic, believe it or not, was the *onion ring*. And I probably told a lot more in my report than people really wanted to know about onion rings. I learned, though, that the onion rings you buy at a place like Burg-O-Rama aren't any more natural than Alfred Nobel's dynamite sticks.

It seems that food researchers (I never knew before that there were such people) discovered that basically many people didn't like onions and therefore weren't buying onion rings. Also, it was difficult to get a machine to peel and slice onions into perfect rings, so they couldn't be mass-produced. To solve that, the researchers invented something new, sort of artificial onion rings. They took onions out of the field, ground them into a paste—stems and all—molded them into things the size of onion rings, covered them with sugary batter, and deep-fried them. These things are mass-produced in a factory, then shipped to the neighborhood Burg-O-Rama, where they are reheated in a microwave.

"Really," I said to the class, "these rings ought to be called onion-flavor doughnuts. They're that sweet, and they hardly taste like onions at all."

"But I like them," Kelly complained.

"Me too," said Bev Harper. "I can't live without them."

"One of the reasons you can't," I told Bev, "is because of all that sugar. It appeals to your sweet tooth and gets you hooked."

Bev could afford to get *un*hooked and drop a few pounds, though I didn't say so.

There were a few more questions and then I sat down, feeling that the report was okay. But other people did fancier jobs on their presentations than I did. Jane Heath is good at art and had spent a lot of time preparing a set of posters showing the basic food groups. Everybody congratulated Jane on the job she did, and it made me wish I'd thought of some sort of display or demonstration. I could have made up some onion rings—fake ones like Burg-O-Rama's, maybe in peculiar shapes or people's initials—and fried them up in an electric skillet.

Kelly Flynn, who always has to be the center of attention, decided she would not be outdone by *anybody*, especially Jane. So the day her report was due, Kelly showed up in a *costume;* she was actually dressed like a *carrot,* wearing a tight pair of orange ski slacks, an orange short-sleeved sweater, and a green felt cowboy hat with a green, fluffy feather in it. I thought she looked ridiculous, but the outfit did show off her body to good advantage. And even I have to admit that she has a terrific figure. Everybody—especially the boys—sat up straighter when she came in wearing that outfit.

It seemed she had attracted somebody else's attention, too, because just before her report, the Big Fella came into the classroom and squeezed down the aisle to set up his cameras in back. He filmed all the way through Kelly's report, which was a weak, empty thing on health foods and vitamins. She must have said "wholesome" about twenty-five times, and it was obvious that she'd spent more time thinking about her costume than her report. She bobbed around a lot, and most of the boys loved the opportunity to look her over as she stood in front of the class.

I looked over at Tom and I could see that he was uneasy about having his girl friend strut her stuff that way. George thought that the whole thing was pretty funny, and he laughed a lot. I caught Jane's eye, and she shook her head; we were both amazed at the length Kelly would go to to try to make herself a star. At the end of the report there was some applause, but no questions, which was probably a good thing because I doubt that Kelly could have answered any.

Despite her efforts, though, Kelly didn't manage to steal the whole show. The real star turned out to be Russell Moffett, a junior who is basically a science nut. I don't think he is involved in any extracurricular activities or clubs, except every year he spends a lot of time preparing science projects to exhibit at the Morgan County Fair. Last year he made a working model of a solar panel that could be used to heat water, and he won a blue ribbon. The year before he built two robots out of cardboard, painted them silver, and wired them with tape recorders so that they seemed to talk to each other. He got a red ribbon for that. Russ is kind of formal and shy, the sort of kid who reads in the lunchroom, usually science fiction. But if you stop to talk to him, he'll carry on a good conversation and show that he's got a sense of humor.

He began his presentation by writing on the chalkboard: YOU ARE WHAT YOU EAT. Then he drew the outline of a hot dog in a bun.

"Do you know what you're eating?" he asked— the whole class, not anybody in particular.

He turned to the board again, and right in the middle of the hot dog, where the meat is, he drew two, sad, forlorn eyes.

We cracked up. That hot dog looked *so* unhappy.

"You laugh," Russ said, without smiling. "But you won't laugh when I'm through telling you about what you're putting in your mouths and bodies."

He walked over to a small speaker's stand that Mr. Walton sometimes uses, but Russ didn't have any notes to put on it—everything seemed to be in his head.

"My report," he said, "is on the federal regulations about food processing, what our government does and doesn't do to make certain that what we eat is 'pure,' 'natural,' and 'healthy.' "

He nodded at me, having quoted my words that set off this whole thing.

"For example," he continued, "I suspect most of you enjoy eating the all-American hot dog."

People nodded, and I heard several boys laughing at the back of the room, probably making dirty remarks about hot dogs. Russ ignored them.

"When you go to the store and buy them—*hot dogs, frankfurters*, or whatever you call them— the package will usually say ALL MEAT. And it's true that the product you buy is mostly meat— usually pork or beef."

He scanned the class slowly, making certain he had our attention.

"What they don't tell you about," he said softly, building up suspense, "is the *snouts*." He practically whispered the word.

"Snouts?" Bev Harper asked aloud, her eyes wide.

Somebody at the back of the room gave a loud snort.

"*Snouts*," Russ emphasized. "Little pink piggie snouts. Wet, drippy moo-cow noses. *Snouts*— ground up into the hot dog meat."

"Oh, yuck," said Dianne Leighton. "Gross."

"Not to mention the jowls." Russ pinched himself on the cheeks. "And the salivary glands, the lymph nodes, and the spleens." He pointed to his throat, his shoulder, his stomach. "It's an old saying in the hot dog industry that they use everything but the oink and the moo."

"You mean they can do that?" George Foley asked. "The government lets them?"

"The government exercises some control," Russ answered. "There are limits on the amount of that stuff they can put in. And to the kind. The government stopped them from grinding up the eyeballs and anuses a few years back."

Somebody groaned, maybe Bev Harper.

"That sounds really awful," Jane said, putting it mildly.

"I will recite a poem on the subject," Russ said, and he sort of stood at attention:

> Oh hot dog makers everywhere,
> How could you be so mean?
> We're all so very sorry
> About your giant grinding machines.
> For all the stray old cats and dogs
> Will never more be seen.
> They'll all be ground to hot dogs
> In those giant grinding machines.

Everybody laughed at that, and Russ bowed. We were enjoying the show, even the grossness, and seeing Russ come out this way. Everybody, that is, except Tom, who still seemed in a funk about Kelly and her costume and was trying to give her the evil eye across the classroom. Kelly was pretending she didn't see him, pretending she was entranced by what Russ was talking about.

"I honestly believe," Russ continued, "that without the small amount of government regulating that goes on, the manufacturers would put in just about everything they could to make hot dogs cheaper. Not too long ago a company got caught putting in fish meal. That's made up of ground fish—bones, tails, skin, and all."

"What happened?" George asked. "What did the government do?"

"Just asked them to stop," Russ replied. "That's about all they really *can* do."

"They should put them in jail," Bev Harper said.

"Or fine them," George said, "and pool the money for something."

"For sure," Jane put in, "they ought to have *some* more power."

"In fact, they do," Russ said. "Our government has the power to supervise the cleanliness of the meat packing plants to make certain the animal hair and feces are kept down to reasonable limits."

"Hair?" Jane asked. "Feces?"

"Reasonable?" I added. "Limits?"

"Yes," Russ answered. "Hair and feces. Limits. You see, it's impossible to keep rats out of the packing plants. There's a lot of garbage around to attract them. And you can't control the rats with poison."

"Why not?" George asked.

"Because the rats might crawl off and die in some of the grinding equipment and wind up in the meat, which would poison us too." He shrugged helplessly. "So the rats have the run of the place and you've got to expect some of their hair and turds in your hot dog."

Russ smiled at us. He was having a good time grossing us out.

"Come on, Russ," Jane said. "Lay off a little." She looked like she was getting sick.

"Okay. Okay. But it's important for you to know these things."

He walked to the board and drew an arrow to the meat part of the hot dog.

"Know this," he said, writing down some numbers. "The typical U.S. government-certified hot dog contains only about 12% protein—that's the stuff that makes you grow. The government will let them put in up to 30% fat—that's the stuff that puts on pounds and gives you heart attacks. Then there's about 56% water, for which you're paying two dollars a pound. And finally, there's 4% other things, mostly soybean flour used to glue the whole mixture together."

He circled the "4%" on the board.

"Oh yes," he added, "and there are certain chemicals added in that four percent, some of them for flavor, some of them to keep the hot dogs from spoiling, some to make them nice and pink. And some of those chemicals—like sodium nitrate—have been shown to cause cancer in rats."

"I hope it's the same rats that leave the turds," George Foley said, getting a laugh.

Mr. Walton came into the discussion for the first time.

"What about other meats, Russ? Didn't you

read up on things like hamburger too? That's an area where we're especially interested." He nodded in the direction of the Big Fella, who was fooling around with his camera and paying no attention.

"Hamburgers are not as bad," Russ said. "Probably because the particles are bigger and you can see what you're eating." He gave us a grim smile, then erased the board and put on a new set of numbers. "Burgers have to be pretty much all beef. The government says they can't add anything like flour, and they can't put in any extra water to make them weigh more."

"What about worms?" George Foley asked.

People laughed, although not George.

"No," George said, turning to us. "I'm serious. I heard there's earthworms added to hamburger meat, especially in fast-food places." He looked up at Russ, appealing his case.

"I heard that too," Russ said, "and in some ways it makes good sense, because earthworms are very high in protein." He paused and looked around the class. "Of course, they're probably a bit gritty to eat."

Bev Harper groaned again.

"Come on, Russ," Jane said. "Cut it out."

"Well, seriously," Russ said, "scientists are investigating earthworms as a possible food source, but nothing will probably happen until the twenty-first century. For the time being, we've got enough food. Besides, earthworms are expensive."

"Expensive?" Doug Ellis asked. "They ought to be dirt cheap." He looked over at George, who shook his head sadly. Bad joke.

"You might think so," Russ said, "but earthworms actually cost about five dollars a pound to raise. That's why you won't find them in hamburgers. Cows are still cheaper than worms."

Mr. Walton, standing on the sidelines, nodded.

"But still," Russ continued, "you might be interested in a cute trick the people at Burg-O-Rama and other fast-food places are trying in order to get additives into their burgers."

Our interest went up another notch, and several people glanced back at Ken Deitrick, who was filming away.

"It seems the no-additives rule applies only to things called *hamburger* or *ground beef*. They can put in other things if they call the product something else."

"Such as?" Jane asked.

"Such as *beef patties*," Russ answered, "which can contain lots of fat, soybeans, and extra water."

He let that register for a moment.

"And which explains why we have the Big Fella."

We couldn't help it. We all turned around, every one of us, and looked at Ken Deitrick, alias the Big Fella. I'm certain he knew we called him that. How could he not know? He looked startled when he realized we were all watching him, and then he grinned, looking embarrassed. I'm not certain he had actually heard what Russ said. He looked down and tinkered with his tripod.

"I mean the *hamburger*," Russ said, clutching an imaginary one in his hands. "What you buy at the restaurant." He was embarrassed too; we all were. But he got himself together. "Or nonburger, you might say."

"Nonburger?" Jane asked. "Please don't start with the worms and rats again."

Russ shook his head.

"No, this has to do with soybeans. It seems the Burg-O-Rama management figured that if they didn't call their hamburgers *hamburgers*, they wouldn't have to make them all beef. That's why they gave them names like Big Fella, Tom Thumb, the Double Dealer—names like that. They figured they could add soybeans and water and extra fat."

"Isn't somebody trying to stop them?" I asked. "I would think the government would. That's really fake, isn't it?"

"It is," Russ answered, "and in Maryland, they're doing something. Their attorney general has sued Burg-O-Rama to make them stop. The case is in court right now. But in the meantime, the burgers you buy at Burg-O-Rama are really *soyburgers*, stuffed like your Thanksgiving turkey."

"Interesting, Russ," Mr. Walton interrupted. He

looked at his watch. "We're already over the time limit, but I sense there is a good deal of interest here, so we can take more time, if needed. Are there any other questions?"

We had plenty to ask, and Russ was really on top of his facts. We asked him about soda pop, and he told us it contains so much sugar and caffeine it can make little kids hyper. We wanted to know about hamburger and hot dog buns, and he explained how the flour is bleached "pure" white and sugar is added for extra sweetness. Someone asked about milk shakes and we learned that they actually contain artificial milk made out of soybeans. We wanted to know if the fish and chicken restaurants were any better than Burg-O-Rama, and he told us about "scavenger" fish and "junk" fish that are sold cheap to fast-food places because nobody else will buy them, and about chickens that are fed dye just before they are killed to make their skin turn golden. Russ kept us interested through most of the class period. Then Mr. Walton jumped in again.

"Thanks, Russ," he said. "That's enough questions for now. Let's see if we can draw some conclusions from this. Can you?" He waved his hand in the general direction of the class.

I had to speak. "To begin with," I said, "I can see why you were on me about that word 'natural.' "

"Which was?"

"Well, obviously what the Burg-O-Rama Man said about '100% natural' was misleading. Their stuff isn't all that natural."

"Or 'pure' or 'healthy'?"

"Or pure or healthy."

"It's deception," George Foley said. "That's all there is to that." He pounded his fist on the desk.

"But does that change your way of thinking about these commercials now, George?" Mr. Walton asked. "Do you have any scruples now?"

The question caught him by surprise, and George shook his head to himself. He wasn't that certain.

"And what about the food itself?" Mr. Walton asked.

"Well," Jane Heath said, "it really *is* junk, isn't it? The stuff is pretty bad for you."

"But it's so-o-o-o good," Bev Harper argued. "How can it be bad for you when it tastes so good?"

"It's obvious," George concluded for us, "that they know how to make it taste terrific so you'll keep on coming back, no matter how bad it may be."

"The question is," Mr. Walton said, "that, knowing what you do about the food, and knowing about what Burg-O-Rama is trying to pull with the names of those hamburgers, whether you will continue to buy there, to eat there. Or at any other junk food place. Will you?"

We were silent, thinking. Nobody really wanted to answer that question. Bad as the stuff was, I know I hated the idea of not ever going there again.

"Aha!" said Mr. Walton, pointing his finger at us.

We still sat there. And in the silence, we suddenly became aware of a person standing at the classroom door, somebody who had been listening to our discussion. The Burg-O-Rama Man.

We knew instantly why he was there, why the Big Fella had been filming. Somebody from this class would be picked to star in a commercial. But who?

The bell rang.

We got up and headed for the door, figuring that somebody was going to be pulled out of the line on the way out.

Kelly got to the door first and gave him a smile that showed every tooth in her head. You could see her slow down, giving him plenty of time to pick her. But he let her go by, and Jane Heath, who was standing next to me, nodded and gave sort of a sniff, glad that Kelly's showing off hadn't worked.

Jane acted quite natural as she went past, giving him an honest hello. She wasn't the one either.

Tom and George went out, Tom not expecting to be picked and hurrying to catch up with Kelly, George kind of wanting to, but figuring he wouldn't be the one. They weren't picked.

Others went by. Russ Moffett went out—I thought maybe he would be the one, but he wasn't. In fact, we *all* went out and were in the hallway, milling around, muttering to ourselves about what was going on.

Then we heard the Burg-O-Rama Man talking from the doorway.

"Mr. Walton," he said, "I hope you will accept an invitation to have lunch with me."

◆ ◆ ◆

OPENING SHOT: From the front steps of Crawford High, looking down the street. An older car pulls up in front of the school.

MUSIC: Orchestra, the Burg-O-Rama theme.

SHOT: Zoom to close-up through car window, passenger side. Robert Walton leans over and kisses his wife. Climbs out of the car, waving to children in the backseat.

ANNOUNCER: Burg-O-Rama would like you to meet Robert Walton.

SHOT: Walton trotting up the steps, carrying a schoolteacher's briefcase.

ANNOUNCER: He is a science teacher at Crawford High School.

SHOTS: Walton in class: standing at the chalkboard, gesturing to make a point, talking with a student about a paper.

ANNOUNCER: As a scientist, Mr. Walton knows about nutrition . . . and his students do too.

SHOTS: Students giving reports: holding up posters, talking to the class, writing on the blackboard about vitamins.

ANNOUNCER: The people at Burg-O-Rama know you are concerned about how your family eats.

SHOTS: Family groups at Burg-O-Rama.

MUSIC: Chorus sings the theme song:

> *Burg-O-Rama, it's a winner.*
> *Take your family there for dinner.*
> *Real good cookin', healthy too,*
> *Burg-O-Rama's the place for you.*

ANNOUNCER: And we want you to know that our whole menu is made up of pure and natural foods.

SHOTS: Close-ups of hamburger, fries, hot dog, fish sandwich, onion rings, soda pop.

ANNOUNCER: Robert Walton and his family know.

SHOT: Mr. and Mrs. Walton and the children in a Burg-O-Rama booth. Table filled with food. Children eating burgers. Mrs. Walton nibbling at a french fry. Walton laughing with kids. Camera zooms in and freezes on his face.

MUSIC: Swells to finish.

SHOT: Burg-O-Rama logo fills the screen, then shrinks to upper-left corner. Announcement appears:

A promotional fee has been paid to the Crawford City, Ohio, Public Schools and to

Mr. Robert Walton by the Burg-O-Rama Foundation, a division of Trimble Enterprises, Inc.

◆ ◆ ◆

I was shocked. And "shocked" is not a word I use very often because it doesn't happen to me very often.

But I was shocked at the commercial because it was such a fake, such a distortion. They'd taken everything we'd learned in Mr. Walton's class and twisted it around to make Burg-O-Rama look like a health food restaurant instead of a junk food store. I knew that none of the commercials they were doing were really true to life, but that one disgusted me.

But I was more shocked that Mr. Walton actually agreed to be in it.

And I wasn't the only one. People were shocked and *angry*.

"I thought they said it was supposed to be kids," Kelly Flynn said at lunch that day. She had gone into a sulk right after class and stayed there.

"Oh, Kelly," Jane said, sounding mother-to-daughter, "you're just mad because you weren't picked. You thought that carrot costume would do it for you, didn't you?"

As a matter of fact, all that costume had got Kelly was trouble, because Tom had decided it showed her off too much and was angry that she had worn it. They had argued and had a big fight in the hall outside Walton's class with everybody watching. That added to Kelly's sulkiness, and Tom had turned sour and wouldn't talk to anyone.

George Foley was angry too.

"Think of all that money. A teacher doesn't need that money. A teacher gets paid to teach. Walton shouldn't be allowed to get the money. Or he should have to share it with the students."

"Teachers need money too," Jane answered him. "Remember what Mr. Walton said once about not making enough money? Now maybe he won't have to quit teaching."

"Who cares?" George said. "It's a crummy thing that Walton's doing."

"Well," Jane said, "I agree that it's fake. After all he said to us about not eating the stuff, here he's going to be selling it."

I thought somebody needed to defend Mr. Walton. "He didn't tell us not to eat that food. He let us draw our own conclusions."

"Maybe," Jane said. "But we *knew* what he thought. It was no mystery."

But what Mr. Walton really thought was a mystery to me, and I was not only puzzled but hurt, because I thought he had let us down.

In the following weeks he seemed to know that people were angry. He never said anything more about the Burg-O-Rama Man or, for that matter, about nutrition. In class we went on and studied reproduction in plants and flowers. Mr. Walton stopped asking us so many questions and didn't tease us or play games with us anymore. He gave us more pop quizzes, and the exams got harder. The class became almost boring, in some ways just as slow as Mr. Pinnavia's history class.

Toward the end of the school year we heard that Mr. Walton had turned in his resignation to the Board of Education. Somebody said that he was going to law school full time in the fall. I was sorry to know he was leaving, because I still think that in most ways he was the best teacher I ever had in four years at Crawford High School.

But I am still shocked that he did the commercial. And if I could talk with him, someplace outside school, when nobody was around and we had some time, I'd really like to ask *him* some questions.

Starting with, "Why?" Especially after all that talk about "Scruples."

CHAPTER

4

Crawford City is pretty much a White Anglo-Saxon Protestant town. I'm a WASP. The Power Mongers are WASPs. Just about all the kids at Crawford High School are WASPs. The only exception is a neighborhood just east of the downtown square that is mostly Italian Roman Catholic. Some people call it Little Italy, though not when anybody who lives there is around. This neighborhood is unusual because you wouldn't expect to find an Italian community in this part of Ohio at all.

The reason for it is that when old Junius P. Crawford opened his mill here a hundred years ago, he brought in a lot of foreign laborers, most of whom were Italian. The people who came liked it here, so the story goes, and they would save up enough money working at the mill to send for their families and bring them over.

When the mill closed years and years ago, some of the Italian people left and moved to Cincinnati and Pittsburgh, but also a lot of them stayed. Some people found other jobs here, while some of them started their own businesses. Over the years people grew up and got married and had kids, who mostly stayed in Crawford City. Everybody over there seems related to everybody else— cousins or grandparents or something—and they've all gone to the Crawford City schools.

As far as neighborhoods go, the Italian section is one of the oldest. It certainly is one of the prettiest too. The houses are tall and narrow, some of them three stories or three stories plus an attic, usually painted white. In the summer everybody has bright flower boxes on their porches, and big old trees arch over the streets and make them shady. By contrast, most of the rest of Crawford is newer houses, built suburbia style, one story, with trees that aren't much more than leafy sticks in the ground.

One Saturday morning toward the end of March I found myself over in the Italian neighborhood more or less by accident. There had been a thaw in the weather and all week it had been sunny and even warm. Although there were still a few piles of blackened snow here and there, mostly it had melted away. The grass was not only showing through, some of it seemed to be turning green, and if you looked carefully in flower beds, you could see some buds pushing up through the dead leaves.

That Saturday the temperature was up in the 60s by midmorning, and I was bored, so I decided to go for a bike ride. I dragged out my bicycle, a one-speed heavyweight I had picked up at a garage sale, and dusted it off. Then I oiled the chain and the brakes and rode down to Shugar's Standard station, where the kid put about two gallons of air into each tire and insulted me by calling my bike a "balloon-tire bomber."

For a while I went riding, just cruising up and down the streets, sort of like I had when I was a kid, even splashing through puddles for the fun of it, getting the kinks out of my bike and me. It was in the Italian section that I realized I was getting hot and tired, so I looked for a place to take a breather and to get something to eat. What I found was Costello's grocery.

It was almost hidden, halfway down a block, right in the middle of a string of white houses. As a matter of fact, it looked like one of the houses itself, converted to a store. Across the front was a faded sign with two big Coca-Cola bottle caps at either end and the name COSTELLO'S MARKET printed in green letters. The front windows were stacked with fruits and vegetables: row after row of apples, oranges, and grapefruits; carrots in bunches all pointing the same way; lettuce heads, damp with little beads of water and sitting in a bed of crushed ice.

I parked the bike in front, out of the way, not locking it. I figured that nobody would want to swipe it, even though it's my treasured antique. I pushed open the door, which rang a little bell attached to a string. A man at the back of the store looked up at me.

As I went through the door, a smell hit me: coffee. Costello's Market was filled with the aroma of coffee. I don't drink the stuff, having had maybe a half-dozen cups in my entire life, always with cream and sugar to kill the taste, but I love the smell. It was not coming from a coffeepot or anything, but from barrels of coffee beans lined up near the front door. Next to them was a coffee grinder, painted red and white, with an old-fashioned picture of a woman holding a cup of coffee up toward you.

Costello's was that kind of place, a place where you could get the real thing, not something frozen or prepackaged. It was an amazing place with all kinds of different food. Against one wall was the Italian food—not just spaghetti, which you'd expect, but a dozen different kinds of noodles and macaroni: things shaped like bird's nests, seashells, green noodles and other things I had never seen or tasted. There was spaghetti, too, but umpteen different kinds, including some that was so long it had to be bent in a U shape before it could be fitted into a box. They had rows of canned tomato paste and tomato sauce with the labels printed in Italian, and big, open spice jars lined two or three shelves, adding to the wonderful smell of the place. There was Italian bread, too, long and short loaves, round loaves, bags of hard rolls, all piled into a rack with an old and faded sign that said, "Wonder Bread."

The other side of the store was a kind of delicatessen with a row of white coolers with glassed-in fronts. One held cheeses; another contained sliced meats and a bunch of salamis; and a third was filled with homemade salads and submarine sandwiches. Last was a cooler full of pastries: iced cookies, fancy cakes sliced and resting in small paper cups, and rolls glazed with honey.

The aisle of the store was crowded with more stuff. There were stacks of gold cans of olive oil, and a table with a display of Italian cookies. Knee-high crocks were pushed up against the coolers and filled with pickles, olives, and red peppers, all sunk in vinegar or some other liquid. Part of the aisle was taken up by three small round tables covered with red-and-white-checked tablecloths. Above the tables, tacked to one of the shelves, was a sign that said, COSTELLO'S CAFFÈ ITALIANO.

At the back of the store was a butcher counter, with cuts of meat in trays. The man was working away chopping up chickens. He was wearing a blue-and-white-striped shirt, a dark necktie, and a long white apron.

"*Buon giorno,*" he said to me.

"Hi," I said back, feeling a little foolish at giving such an American greeting in such an Italian place. "I just came in for a snack."

He said nothing, but opened his hands in a kind of wave and invitation. The place was mine, he seemed to say.

I browsed through the fruit in the front window and picked out an apple that looked good, then checked the cookie display and chose a small package of Neapolitan wafers. I paid the man and sat down at one of the tables to enjoy the food, keeping myself busy by trying to figure out a recipe written in Italian on the back of a box of rigatoni.

It was about that time that I saw Mary Costello coming out of the back room, tying on an apron.

I suppose I could have guessed or suspected that she was related to the people who ran the store, though there were a lot of Costellos in town and I couldn't really have known that Mary was this Costello. Besides that, I didn't know her very well. She was a junior, and I had taken only a couple of classes with her: one in economics and one in advanced algebra. Mary was a very shy girl. She almost never spoke in class and spent all her time taking notes, listening carefully to what was going on. Not talking didn't seem to cause her any problems with grades, though. I had seen a couple of her test scores in algebra, and they were tops.

Mary was dark—both hair and complexion—and tiny, perhaps five feet two, with a trim body —petite, as they say. Though she was quiet, she wasn't aloof or anything like that. She simply went about her business, not bothering anybody.

She went about her business that Saturday in the grocery, though I think my being there bothered her. When she spotted me, she nodded and gave me a quick smile, but she may have been puzzled as to why I was there and didn't know quite whether to come over and talk to me or not. If that was a problem, though, it was solved when the front door opened, the bell rang, and an old woman came in.

This woman was not just old; she was *ancient*. She walked very slowly, bent over, leaning heavily on a cane. As she went by me, I could see that her face was dry and creased with thousands of wrinkles. Her hair, which was pulled back in a bun, was absolutely white.

Mary came to life in a way that I'd never seen in school.

"*Ciao*, Mrs. Barberio," she said, and she burst into a string of Italian.

The old lady answered her back in Italian, and they carried on a conversation, with Mary cheery and bright, the old lady grumbling like she was complaining. Then slowly—very slowly—the woman pulled a piece of paper out of her purse and began to give Mary an order.

Mrs. Barberio must have wanted about nine or ten things out of the delicatessen cases, just a little bit of each one. She took forever to make up her mind, spending a long time just staring into the glass or at her list and not saying anything. Sometimes she would point to something, and Mary would get a cheese or a tray out for her to look at. A couple of times she changed her mind after seeming to decide.

When the lady finally made up her mind, Mary would swing into action. She'd pick up a big sausage or cheese and smack it onto a slicer, tear a sheet of white waxed paper off a roll and set it down under the machine, cut a few slices, weigh them on a scale, cut off some more, fold the paper, zip some brown paper tape off a dispenser, slap that on the package, pull a black grease pencil out of her apron pocket, write down the amount, and plunk the package down with all the others on top of the deli counter. Then she'd look over at the old lady.

"Anything else, Mrs. Barberio?" she'd say, sometimes in English, usually in what I figured was the same question in Italian.

Mrs. Barberio thought and thought, looking around the place to see if she'd forgotten anything. It would have absolutely driven me up the wall to wait on her, but Mary kept smiling through it all.

Finally the woman muttered something—"No more," I suppose—and gave a jerky wave of the hand as if to say, "Enough!" She turned and headed for the door without as much as saying "Thank you," leaving her packages on the counter. I wanted to say, "Hey, lady, you forgot your stuff" (including forgetting to pay for it), but Mary just scooped up all the packages and dropped them in a brown paper bag, which she marked with a grease pencil and put in a deli case. Apparently Costello's delivered. And had charge accounts.

There was a lull after the woman left. Mary spoke to the man at the butcher counter, then came over to see me, wiping her hands on a towel. Somebody had embroidered "Costello's" in bright red thread across the top of her apron.

"Hello, Karen," she said, still shy.

"Hi, Mary," I answered. "Nice to see you."

She didn't say anything, so I felt I needed to carry on the conversation. "I was just out for a bike ride and stopped by for a little something to eat." I felt uncomfortable and pointed to my apple core and the cookie wrappers as if to back up my story. "I really like your store."

Mary seemed pleased, but "thanks" was all she said.

The man called from behind the butcher counter.

"Go ahead; take a break, Mary. Sit down and talk with your friend."

Mary pulled up a wire chair, though I could see that she wondered if I really wanted her to talk.

"I didn't know about this place," I said, still making conversation. "I mean, there's nothing like it anyplace in Crawford City."

"I know," she said. "It's Papa's pride and joy." She gestured in the direction of the man. "It was his idea to do it over this way."

"Over?"

"Yeah. It hasn't always been like this. When Papa was a boy—when *his* father owned the store —it was just a neighborhood grocery with a small section of Italian food. When Papa took over, he decided to make it all Italian."

"Well, it seems a lot better this way," I said.

"To me too," Mary added, "though I was much too young to remember the store the other way."

Of course. How could I have known which way was better? I was too young, too, and had never been in the place before that day. Still, it *seemed* better, so I nodded in agreement.

I looked around at the shelves. "Where do you get all this stuff? Do you have to send all the way to Italy for it?"

She laughed quietly. "No. But we do have to send for it. Most of the Ohio food distributors don't carry real Italian food, so we get it shipped in from New York City."

"That's great," I said. "I'll bet people around here, I mean in this area . . . this neighborhood . . . appreciate it." I was mumbling and stumbling for words because I wasn't going to say, "Little Italy."

"Lots do," she replied, "but a lot of people have forgotten."

"Forgotten what?"

"Their background. They've lived in Ohio for so long they've lost touch. Papa says he has to teach some of our neighbors to be Italian all over again. Like, he has recipes printed up using original ingredients. Otherwise a lot of people would buy bottled sauce and American pasta. He shows them how to do it the old way."

"That's neat." I thought for a moment. "You know, it makes me realize I don't have anything like that, like an ethnic background."

As a matter of fact, I'm a mongrel. I know I've got some Scottish-Irish in me and some German, and I have a genuine Dutch uncle, but the bloodlines are so mixed that I'm not really anything. I have no sense of my roots, other than the fact that I'm an Ohioan—and what's that?

"Papa has stressed our Italian roots ever since we were kids," Mary said. "He's taught us some Italian and told us stories about 'the old country,' even though he's never lived there and got them all from his father."

"I wondered about your Italian," I said. "I didn't think you could learn to talk it that way in school."

Our foreign language classes are really bad, and everybody knows it.

"That's just a little basic conversation," Mary explained. "I doubt that I could do much if we actually got to Italy. But we talk it around the store a lot, and all the neighbors can talk with one another, and Papa even makes me practice when no customers are here."

"You spend a lot of time here," I said, rather than asked, because it was obvious.

"Yeah, pretty much. I work after school and on Saturdays. Sometimes on Sundays for a while, though we're closed."

"It must be tough to get your schoolwork done. How do you find time?"

"Well," she said, "I do most of my homework in school. I pretend to be taking notes in class, but I actually work on the next day's assignment while the teacher talks."

Aha. A trade secret. I was impressed. She had to be really smart to carry that off, looking alert in class while thinking about and doing something else.

The bell on the door rang, and a customer came in. It was another old lady, somebody who could have been the sister of Mrs. Barberio—white hair in a bun the same way, hunched over the same way, only not using a cane.

"*Buon giorno*, Mrs. Filipelli," Mr. Costello called from the butcher counter.

The old lady just grunted in reply.

Mary stood up. *"Buon giorno,"* she said to the woman. "I gotta go," she said to me. "It was nice talking to you."

"It was really nice talking to *you*," I said.

Mary started to walk toward the old woman, but turned back to me and said, "You know, if you're interested in this"—she waved at the shelves, the store—"you might enjoy coming to the Italian Festival. It's next Tuesday night over at St. Anthony's. There's a sign about it in the window."

"Thanks," I said, spotting the poster. "I'll think about it."

I picked up my apple core and cookie wrapper and looked for a place to toss them. I didn't see a basket, so I stuffed them in my pocket and headed for the door.

"So long," Mary said.

"Ciao," I tried, my first Italian ever.

She grinned and nodded her approval, then turned to the old woman. "How can I help you, Mrs. Filipelli?"

St. Anthony's Church has always been a place of great mystery and almost fear for me. When I was younger, I went to Methodist Sunday school. I don't think they tried to prejudice us against Catholics or anything like that, but they did tell us about some practices that sounded pretty strange and made us all glad we were Methodists.

St. Anthony's Church itself is really quite pretty, a red brick church with a gray, slate-covered roof. It could be a Protestant church, except for the fact that there is a statue of the Virgin Mary on the front lawn. In the summer-time she is in the middle of a rose garden, and if you go by, you can sometimes see the priests taking care of the flowers. In the winter they put up a wooden shed over the Virgin, and at Christmas-time there is a nativity scene in the shed, complete with the manger, animals, shepherds, wise men, and the same Virgin, looking down at the baby Jesus. The church is lit up with red and green floodlights, and the inside lights are left on so the stained glass windows shine out into the winter night. It is all very pretty.

But who knew what went on inside the church?

So it was with some nervousness that I thought about going to the Italian Festival at St. Anthony's. I made a couple of calls to see if any of the Power Mongers wanted to come with me. George was busy. He'd joined a karate club at the Y and he was spending Tuesday nights learning to chop bricks in half with his bare hands—or so he said.

"That's a useful skill," I told him, "especially if you're thinking about being a bricklayer."

George also said that Tom and Kelly would be busy. They were supposedly going over to the library to work on a history report. I doubted that they'd ever make it to the library, and for sure, no history would be reported on, but they weren't free to go to the festival. When I reached Jane, she said she had been planning to work on the same history report at home, but she could finish it later, and sure, the Italian Festival sounded like fun. Besides, she reminded me, we'd been so busy in recent weeks that we'd hardly had a chance to get off alone, away from the others, just to catch up on our conversation.

The night was clear and not too cold, so we decided to walk and talk. I reached her house about seven, just as it was getting dark, and we headed off for St. Anthony's, a mile or so away. We chit-chatted about school and assignments for a while. The Burg-O-Rama Man came up in our conversation and we wondered a bit about who would be picked next, and whether it would be any of the Power Mongers.

"I wish Tom would get it," Jane said. "It would do him a lot of good."

"What's going on with him anyway?" I asked. "He sure has turned into a crab lately."

Jane walked along silently for several sidewalk squares, and I thought at first she wasn't going to answer. I was about to change the subject to George Foley and karate when she finally spoke.

"As a matter of fact, I think Tom thinks he's . . . over the hill."

I laughed out loud, which was not in good taste since Jane is so fond of him.

"Over the hill? The guy's only seventeen years old and built like a Greek god. He's got a couple hundred thousand miles left on him."

"I don't mean it that way," she answered, and to be truthful, I knew that wasn't what she meant. "It's just that he feels left out of things these days, like his time of glory is over, like there's not a lot left for him at Crawford."

I could see what she meant. Sports had been everything for Tom, and now with football over and senior year running out, he had earned his last letter.

"And he's worried."

"About what?"

"Next year."

"In what way?"

"For one thing," she said, "of all the Mongers, he's the only one who isn't going on to college."

That was right. Jane was thinking about women's schools in the East; George wanted to go to Ohio State; I was checking out small colleges in the Midwest; and even Kelly was going to go someplace, probably OSU or Cincinnati. Only Tom wasn't talking about going away next year.

"He used to think about it," I said. "Why has he dropped the idea?"

"Because the big football schools didn't recruit him. I tried to talk to him about it. I told him sports wasn't the end of the world." Jane sighed. "I told him he could try out even though he didn't have a scholarship, or maybe he could play in intramurals."

"What did he say to that?"

"Nothing. He wouldn't even answer me."

We walked on in silence for a few more squares.

"What about Kelly?" I asked after a bit.

"What about her?"

"Couldn't she talk to Tom? Can't she help him understand?"

Jane gave me a funny look, and I realized I'd hurt her feelings.

"I don't really think Kelly cares that much," she said, "and that's another thing that bothers me."

Up to this time she hadn't actually said that *anything* bothered her, so I listened closely—the Girl Reporter about to get her Best Friend's Deep Secret.

"Even though Kelly says she's 'hopelessly in love' with Tom"—Jane imitated Kelly's voice and I smiled— "I think she's actually looking forward to being on the loose next year with all those college guys to choose from. I figure she'll be picked up by some fraternity guy about twenty minutes after she sets foot on a college campus."

"Yeah," I said. "Too bad." Too bad that somebody like her would be such hot stuff on campus. Too bad she was hurting Tom.

"Stop me if it's none of my business," I said

cautiously, "but I just think it's too bad that Tom doesn't realize he could have you . . . be with you . . . if he wanted. I don't understand why you are so loyal to him. What is it with you and Tom anyway?"

A lot of people would have dodged that question or pretended they didn't understand it or said, "What do you mean 'What is it?' " Jane gave me a straight answer.

"I'm not sure I understand it myself," she said quietly. "It's just that as long as I've known him— ever since grammar school—I've had a crush on him. I just think he's . . . a really nice person."

"But you're still just friends."

"Just friends. I don't think Tom even knows how much I like him."

"He should know," I said, "and he should know that you could have your pick of just about any guy at Crawford High School."

"Well, maybe," she said with a sad smile, "except for Tom."

"Then Tom is just dumb," I said loudly into the empty street, sounding kind of dumb myself. Then more quietly: "But still, why haven't you dated some of the others?"

"The others? There's not much to choose from around Crawford, I'm afraid."

I thought that was easy for her to say, since she had her pick. Nobody was beating a path to my door, so maybe I wasn't as critical of the Crawford High guys.

"Sometimes," Jane continued, "I think I'm a little like Kelly."

"What!?" I couldn't imagine how.

"Well, when I think about next year, I just think that the guys at college will be more interesting than the ones around here. Not that I'm going to college mainly to catch a guy."

We both nodded vigorously. I knew what she meant.

"But," she said, "maybe I'm just like Kelly and I'll fall for the first fraternity guy who comes along."

"Hah," I replied. "If anybody tries to sweep you off your feet, it will be one of the professors— some guy smoking a pipe, with patches on the elbows of his tweed coat, who'll say, 'Ah, yes, my dear' all the time."

She enjoyed that, and we both relaxed.

"But seriously," I said, "what *will* Tom be doing next year? Does he have any plans?"

She frowned, and I thought maybe I should just have dropped it.

"He doesn't really know. He talked to some people over at the health spa in the mall. Maybe they'll let him be an instructor—he's got the build for it."

"Hmmmmm" was all I could think of to say.

"Yeah," she agreed. "That might be okay for a while, but it's not a *life*."

We grew silent again. I couldn't think of anything else to say, and Jane either couldn't or didn't want to. I hoped talking about Tom hadn't depressed Jane and wouldn't ruin the festival for us, and as we turned the last corner and saw the St. Anthony Parish Hall all lit up in the night, my nervousness returned.

I don't know just what I had expected to see at St. Anthony's, maybe crucifixes hung up everyplace with the bleeding Jesus looking down at me wherever I went. Instead, Jane and I found an ordinary gymnasium with basketball hoops hung at either end and a big scoreboard with wire mesh nailed over it to protect it from basketballs. The gym had been decorated with long streamers of red, green, and white crepe paper, and cafeteria-type tables were arranged into stalls or booths around the sides of the gym, each one covered with a red, white, and green tablecloth. Every booth was selling something, and under the scoreboard a band was warming up.

The place was packed with people of all ages. Little kids were running around loose; clusters of teen-agers, mostly kids I didn't know, were standing around here and there; young, middle-aged, and old couples were going around checking out the booths. Jane and I paid our dollar admission, signing our names on the back of the tickets to give us a chance on winning a new Oldsmobile.

For a while we wandered around looking at the booths. Some of them were selling food; others had games you could play for prizes. We went by the Fish Bowl, where little kids paid a quarter and dropped a fishing line into a fake tank and—we could see from the side—a man tied inexpensive toys on the line and gave a sharp tug so it seemed like the fisher had a bite.

There was a T-shirt table where you could get your name embossed on the back of a shirt that said, KISS ME, I'M ITALIAN. I had seen the same kind of shirt for sale at K mart, only it said, KISS ME, I'M POLISH. I noticed the label of one of the shirts and it read, MADE IN TAIWAN.

A sign on the wall advertised a crafts booth, and we pushed through the crowd to see what they were selling. It turned out to be not particularly Italian. They had wooden signs with supposedly funny sayings on them, the kind you hang on the bathroom door when you are using it.

"Just the sort of thing George would appreciate," Jane said.

"I'm glad he's not here," I answered. "He'd probably try to embarrass us."

I looked around for Mary Costello and saw that she and her dad—her papa—had tried to make their booth Italian. They had brought out the round tables from the store and set up a black railing to make what looked like a sidewalk café. The sign from the store, COSTELLO'S CAFFÈ ITAL-IANO, was hung up on the wall. They were brewing coffee, *espresso*, in a big machine that looked like a steam engine, and they had pastries for sale.

Mary and Mr. Costello were really hustling— Mary clearing tables, Mr. Costello making coffee and serving up the pastries. Two women were sitting on folding chairs at the back of the booth, and I guessed they were Mary's mother and grandmother. I could see the family resemblance, though her mother was quite heavy and her grandmother was another of the white-haired, wrinkled types. They weren't doing anything to help, just sitting and talking as if they were at home.

Costello's Caffè Italiano was filled with people and there was a waiting line, so I decided not to bother Mary with conversation. I just waved, and she smiled back.

"Who's that?" Jane asked.

"Just a girl I know," I answered. "Mary Costello. She's a junior. Haven't you seen her around?"

"Maybe," Jane said, "but I'm not sure."

"Sometime let me introduce you. I think you'd like her."

Next door to the Caffè they were selling pizza. The line was moving fast, so Jane and I decided to eat there. When we got to the front, I saw they were unpacking the pizza from cardboard boxes and heating it up, in a radar range. The boxes said SPEEDY PIZZA and had a drawing of a guy in a chef's hat and Italian curved moustache, wearing jogging shoes and running with a pizza in his hand. What they were doing was reheating fast food, junk food, that they'd bought out at the Speedy Pizza near the mall.

I was hungry, though, and we bought two slices from a woman in a KISS ME, I'M ITALIAN T-shirt. The stuff was steaming hot, and the radar range had melted the cheese onto the paper plate. When I tried to pick up the slice, the cheese slid right off, making a mess. As I was wrestling with long strings of mozzarella cheese and burning myself on the hot sauce, I looked up and saw Mary Costello watching me with a slight smile on her face. She shrugged; I looked at the glop in my hands and shrugged back. Then she went back to work, pouring refills of coffee for people crowded around one of the tables. I pitched the pizza in a trash can and licked the sauce and cheese off my fingers. It tasted like cardboard.

The band started to play, a group of six guys. I hate to make value judgments about how people look, but they *looked* Italian, with dark skin and eyes and hair. But instead of Italian music, they played rock—top-forty stuff—with amplified guitars that added to the din of the festival. A few of the high school kids started to dance, but most people just watched.

An older guy, maybe twenty-five, came over to us and asked Jane if she wanted to dance. He was a really good-looking guy, slender and dark, wearing a tight-fitting black shirt, open at the throat, and he seemed very confident. Jane turned him down, and he started to argue with her, with a "C'mon, baby" line. I moved away to give her some space, and she said something that got rid of the guy. When she was free, we exchanged glances that said the same thing, and we headed for the door, both wanting to get out of there. We didn't even wait for the drawing on the Oldsmobile, which would have made George Foley mad. The Italian Festival had been a big disappointment to me. Except for the Caffè, I hadn't seen anything that looked truly Italian.

The next day I saw Mary in the lunchroom. She was by herself, so I thought I'd join her, skipping my usual luncheon engagement with the Mongers. Mary was eating something out of a delicatessen container.

"What have you got there?" I asked as I pulled out a chair. "Looks good."

"Oh, hi, Karen." She wiped her mouth on a napkin. "Antipasto salad. I made up a batch at the store this morning and thought it would be good for lunch."

"This morning? You were working at the store before school?"

"For a little while. I usually go in about 6:30 to make whatever deli recipes we need for the day, then head off for school."

"You amaze me," I said. "I don't know how you get the energy to do it, especially after you worked at the festival the night before—worked hard!"

"I don't really mind it. It's kind of nice to be up early and at the store when everything is quiet."

She continued eating her salad. I started in on my own sumptuous lunch: a homemade peanut butter sandwich and a banana that turned out to be bruised and half-rotten.

She broke the silence. "I'm sorry I built up the festival for you. It wasn't very good, I'm afraid."

"Oh, sure it was," I said, but not very convincingly.

"It's not always that bad," Mary said. "Or, at least, it wasn't until a couple of years ago. It used to be better."

"How?"

"More authentic. Less junk. The women used to do a lot of home cooking and baking. It was neat —you could buy a sampler plate and taste everybody's favorite dishes, and the St. Anthony's Guild would print a cookbook with the recipes."

"Well, at least you and your dad were selling the real thing."

"But we were the only ones. I saw that pizza you got."

It was my turn to apologize. "I only got it because you seemed really busy."

"I know." She toyed with some curious-looking vegetable in her salad. "Papa was furious that they sold Speedy Pizza instead of making it fresh. He's going to complain to the festival committee."

"Do you think it will do any good?"

"Probably not. Speedy Pizza sold it cheap to the church, and I heard the pizza booth made more than any other. They won't want to change, especially since the church needs the money."

"It sounds like a losing battle," I said. "I hate to be discouraging, but why do you and your dad keep it up? I mean, it would probably have been simpler if you didn't drag your tables out to the church and sold regular coffee instead of *espresso*."

"I don't exactly know," she answered, "except that we like to do it. We think it is important."

She really did mean *we*. It was not just Mr. Costello who was pushing the ethnic thing; Mary was into it just as much as he was.

"You're your father's daughter," I said, smiling at her. "It's as simple as that."

"I guess that's right," Mary replied, looking at me with an expression that showed she had never thought of the idea before. "I'm proud of that," she said.

And then, Mr. Costello died.

I heard about it at school the first thing the next

Monday morning. A girl told me, "Some kid's father died." But it wasn't until later in the day that I learned it was Mary Costello's dad.

Nobody knew much about what had happened, except that he had collapsed at work—at the store —Saturday afternoon and was dead by the time they got him to the hospital. Everybody thought it was a heart attack.

The Crawford *Sentinel* printed a short obituary, giving information about the funeral at St. Anthony's and listing Mr. Costello's survivors: a wife, Rose; two sons, Vincent, twenty-five, of Palatine, Illinois, and Joseph, twenty-two, of Albany, New York; a daughter, Mary, sixteen, a junior at Crawford High School. Mr. Costello had been only forty-nine years old.

I didn't go to the funeral, though I thought about it a lot. I figured that in the first place, I didn't really know Mr. Costello that well, and second, it would probably be a funeral for the family and the Italian community. Probably I was a little scared of going to a Catholic funeral at St. Anthony's, but I don't think that influenced my decision about not going.

I did send a card. Jane came with me to the card shop to find one that was appropriate. A lot of them had messages that we really thought were bad and not comforting at all to somebody whose father had just died. Eventually I settled on one that just said, "With deepest sympathy," which was the way I felt for Mary. I signed my full name, figuring that "Karen" alone might not mean anything to her.

For several days I was sad and upset by it all, worried about Mary, and at the same time wondering what I would do if the same thing had happened to me. It was the first time I'd ever known of something like that, somebody close to a person I knew dying, and I didn't know what to think.

Mary was out of school for a week. I checked the absence list each day, and in fact, the day she came back she had been marked absent, so she must have arrived late. I saw her by chance while I was on my free hour, running around on newspaper business. She was in the hall outside the main office, sitting on a cement bench that is built right into the wall. When kids are in trouble and have to see Dr. McCollom, they have to wait on that bench. It's called "the Hot Seat," and almost nobody sits there voluntarily, even just to rest. Mary had her books stacked up beside her, but she wasn't reading or anything.

I walked over to her.

What do you say to a person who has been through something like that? You can't act like nothing happened, but you don't want to upset the person any more than she has been already.

Can you say the word "death" around them? I didn't know.

"Hello, Mary," I said, and she looked up. "I was sorry to hear about your father." That didn't seem to be enough, so I took her hand.

"Thank you, Karen. I got your card."

She looked awful. Tired, and thinner about the face, as if she'd lost weight, and she didn't need to lose weight.

I stood there holding her hand. Neither of us said anything. I felt really awkward.

"Well," I finally said, "I'm glad to see you're back."

I sounded really hollow to myself. Why would a kid whose father had just died care about school at all—or care whether somebody cared that she was back?

"I'm not back for long," she said, and she gestured to the pile of books next to her. "I'm just here to see Dr. McCollom and turn these in. I'm quitting school."

"Why?" I asked, astonished. I sat down next to her on the bench. "You're such a good student. Why do you want to quit?"

"I don't really want to," she answered, "but it's the store. There's nobody to run it now. I have to be there full time."

"But," I sputtered, "but, you can't do it alone. That's too much. Can't somebody else do it?"

"Who?" she asked. "Mama doesn't know anything about the business. Vinnie and Joe, my brothers, have moved away. I'm the only one left."

"But," I sputtered some more, "what about your education? You can't drop out. You shouldn't drop out."

"Why not? I'm not really learning anything here."

"But what about your future?" I sounded like a counselor, I know. "I mean, if you don't get your diploma, you can't do anything."

She gave me an odd look, and I realized I'd said something wrong.

"My future is Mama and the store," she said. "Mama can't get a job at her age. She has no skills except raising a family. She's got to depend on me and the store for a living."

I backpedaled. "I didn't mean to say that the store is *no* future. But aren't there other ways to support your mother?" I thought for a moment. "Like, what if you sold the store? She could probably live off the money and you could finish school."

She gave me another peculiar look, and I realized that I'd blown it again.

"I'd never sell the store. When Vinnie and Joe came back for the funeral, they told Mama the same thing—to sell it—and we had a big fight."

She shook her head with the memory.

"The store has been in our family for three gencrations. I told them I would never let them sell it, not that I could stop them if they really wanted to."

She looked at me, her eyes dark and full of tears.

"How could they even think about selling it with Papa just dead? He loved that place so much."

She began to cry, and I put my arm around her. We sat there for a long time. Eventually she stopped crying and found a tissue in her purse and dried her eyes.

I was feeling clumsy and useless, but I thought I'd try one more time.

"It's really none of my business," I said, "but I really think you should try to finish school if you can. Maybe what you learn isn't that important, but graduating is. And I can't really imagine that you will run the store for the rest of your life."

She looked up at me and nodded slightly, but I could see that I wasn't being very persuasive. I kept going anyway.

"Couldn't you get somebody to tend the store for you during school hours? If you could just get a person for then, you could take over after school and Saturday, same as usual, and still graduate."

She nodded over her shoulder toward the office. "I figure that's what Dr. McCollom will say when he tries to talk me out of it. But the fact is, we can't afford the help. We're not like Giantway, where people spend a hundred dollars a week on groceries and they can even hire kids to carry your bags to the car. We sell a little bit at a time. I just can't afford to hire somebody outside the family to take care of the place."

I had nothing to say and just looked down at my feet, trying to think of something else.

"And besides," Mary continued, and her voice grew stronger, "I don't know that I would trust anybody else to do it. That's why I want to do it. I *must* do it."

We sat there. I'd run out of arguments. I was convinced she was wrong, but I couldn't figure out what to say. Besides, why should she listen to me?

As we sat there, we both realized at the same moment that somebody else was in the corridor, someone standing across from us by the drinking fountain. I don't know how long he'd been there, but when he saw that we'd seen him, the Burg-O-Rama Man came over.

"This probably isn't the best time, Miss Costello," he said, "but I wonder if you and I could have a discussion?"

◆ ◆ ◆

OPENING SHOT: Library. A person seen from in back, seated at a library table, surrounded by books.

MUSIC: The Burg-O-Rama theme hummed by a men's glee club—the sound of a school anthem.

ANNOUNCER: Burg-O-Rama would like you to meet one of Crawford High School's straight-A students.

SHOT: The camera pans around the library table, showing the person from the side, then the front, zooming in slowly to pick up the face, deep in concentration.

ANNOUNCER: Her name is Mary Costello.

SHOT: Mary looks up from her books, as if she had heard the announcer, and smiles shyly at the camera.

ANNOUNCER: Mary works hard at her studies.

SHOTS: A series of Mary in class: writing in her notebook, filling out an answer sheet, punching a calculator, talking with a teacher, studying a fat book.

ANNOUNCER: But that doesn't mean she doesn't have time for other activities.

SHOT: Costello's Market from the outside. The camera zooms in and the front door opens, showing the inside of the store.

ANNOUNCER: Mary is the third generation of her family to work in the family store in Crawford City, Ohio.

MUSIC: An accordion joins the chorus; music changes to a European sound.

SHOTS: Mary behind the counter wearing a Kiss Me, I'm Italian T-shirt. Waiting on a customer. Chopping up cabbage for a salad. Laughing with someone off camera.

ANNOUNCER: Mary and her mother and her grand-mother know . . .

SHOT: The Crawford City Burg-O-Rama.

ANNOUNCER: . . . that Burg-O-Rama can be enjoyed by one generation . . .

SHOT: Close-up of Mary's grandmother, eyeing a big hamburger.

ANNOUNCER: . . . after another . . .

SHOT: Camera draws back to show Mary's mother, also with a hamburger.

ANNOUNCER: . . . after another.

SHOT: Camera backs off still farther to get Mary in the picture, also with a burger. All three start to take a bite at the same time. Freeze.

MUSIC: Chorus, accompanied by accordion, sings:

> *Burg-O-Rama's Number One.*
> *Young or old, you'll think it's fun.*
> *Snack or meal, you'll fill your plate.*
> *Burg-O-Rama's simply great.*

SHOT: Burg-O-Rama logo fills the screen, then shrinks to upper-left corner. Announcement appears:

A promotional fee has been paid to the Crawford City, Ohio, Public Schools and to Mary Costello by the Burg-O-Rama Foundation, a division of Trimble Enterprises, Inc.

◆ ◆ ◆

The kids at Crawford were surprised that Mary was picked for a commercial. Most of them didn't know who she was, and they were puzzled that she had been chosen. When they learned that it was her father who died, though, they agreed she was a good choice. Even George Foley, who had grumbled about every other selection, said that Mary was an okay pick, although he wondered if they had chosen her because they felt sorry for her.

As a matter of fact, I wondered about that, too, since Mary was not the kind of person who ordinarily caught someone's eye, especially an outsider like the Burg-O-Rama Man. Not that she wasn't attractive, but she was so quiet you'd think she was invisible. I guess it made me feel good about the Burg-O-Rama Man that he had spotted what a special person she was.

George also said he heard that Burg-O-Rama had paid her the money in advance so she could stay in school. I didn't know about that, and I certainly wasn't going to ask Mary, though George wanted me to. I know that Mary did change her mind and decided to stay in school. She found somebody she trusted to take care of the store during hours, and she ran it herself the rest of the time, still keeping up her school grades.

As the spring wore on, Mary became happy again—or at least, happier. She looked better and acted more cheerful, and when I saw her, I told her so.

"Yes," she said, "I am happy. As much as I miss Papa, I guess I'm happy. I still don't see that school is doing me any good, but I know he would have wanted me to stick it out and keep up my grades." I nodded, because I knew she was right and I was happy for her. "But my future is that store, and as soon as I graduate, that's where I'm going to spend all my time."

She looked at me and thought for a moment.

"You know," she said, "there's something you said before that I've thought a lot about in the past few weeks."

"What's that?"

"I guess I really am my father's daughter."

CHAPTER
5

After the basketball season there's usually a lull around Crawford High, even during a state championship year. It's too rainy and cold for baseball and the other spring sports, and it's too early for people to get serious about proms and graduation. Classes get to the point where nobody believes they'll ever end, including the teachers, and the spring vacation is maybe a month away. It's a time when the kind of kids who get in trouble get into the most trouble, and I personally find it a bore. There is so little happening around school that I'm tempted to shut down the *Tiger Eye* for a couple of weeks or print issues with blank pages.

The thing that keeps me going is the Drama Club, which goes into rehearsal for its spring play. They usually do a Broadway-type musical and make it a big production. Every kid in the school who dreams of being on stage auditions for a part.

I tried out only once—freshman year, when they did *The Pajama Game*. You had to read a few lines, sing something from a popular song, and do a couple of dance steps while Mr. Gurzenda, the drama teacher, and a bunch of seniors sat in the auditorium, back in the dark where you could hardly see them, and evaluated. In one awful half hour I learned that I can't act, can't sing, and can't dance. I just couldn't let loose and ham it up the way you have to. Almost everybody who tried out got some kind of part, even if it was only being part of the chorus or standing beside a fake sewing machine pretending to make pajamas. I was so bad they wouldn't even let me on stage, so they assigned me to the stage crew, where I raised and dimmed the lights, played the tapes for the sound effects, and had the great honor of pulling the curtain (not a small job, actually, because *The Pajama Game* was a big hit and the kids had to come back for three curtain calls).

That play taught me to love musical theater, even though I'm doomed to spend my life as a curtain puller. So each spring I join the Drama Club for the musical. After four years I can do just about everything connected with production, from making props and scenery to even helping kids with makeup.

This year we were doing *Cabaret*, which, if you like musical theater, you know is a very sophisti-

cated play. Mr. Gurzenda told us he didn't know
of another high school where they had tried it.
Basically, the show is about Germany just before
World War II, and much of it takes place in a
cabaret, or nightclub. While there's a lot of funny
stuff that goes on in the club, it's also kind of
frightening, because you realize that the war is
coming and there are men—Gestapos—hanging
around keeping an eye on people even when
they're having a good time. In *Cabaret* nothing is
ever quite what it seems to be, and if you do the
show right—or at least, if you do it the way Mr.
Gurzenda wanted us to—the audience is fooled
quite a bit.

For instance, at one place in the second act
there's a chorus line on stage with their backs to
you. They're dressed in short skirts and have old-
fashioned stockings with a seam up the back.
When they wheel around to face the audience,
you realize that the girl in the middle is not a girl,
but a guy, the Master of Ceremonies, who winks
at the audience and shakes his finger as if to say,
"Tricked you!"

It's that part of the Master of Ceremonies that
explains why high school groups are afraid to try
Cabaret. The emcee is a very difficult role. He is
everywhere and does everything. He pops up all
over the place at unexpected moments. Sometimes
he dances and sings; other times he has more serious parts. He talks to the audience through the

whole show, telling them what's going on or setting them up for a gag. For the show to work,
you've got to have a boy who's a real superstar
for the part, who's not afraid to do crazy things
like dressing up like a chorus girl. As Mr. Gurzenda said, not very many high schools have a guy
who can do that.

Crawford High School did. His name was—is—
Donnie Hamilton, and everybody agreed that the
part was absolutely made for him. Donnie had
been taking dancing lessons ever since he was a
little kid in first or second grade. By fifth grade he
was too good to be in the Crawford City dancing
class, and the teacher told his parents to send him
to an instructor in Cincinnati. So every Saturday
for eight years Donnie made the trip down and
back for his dancing lessons, and it had paid off,
because he was terrific. Everybody was certain he
could make it as a professional dancer on Broad-
way or TV, and that's the kind of thing he wanted
to do for a career. In my mind there was no doubt
that Mr. Gurzenda had picked *Cabaret* just because of Donnie. It was the last show Donnie
would be in before he graduated, and Mr. Gurzenda wanted it to be the best show in the history
of Crawford.

So, late in March they went into rehearsal, and
to beat the blahs, I joined the stage crew again. (I
told Mr. Gurzenda I was going to get in shape for
curtain pulling by hanging one hour a day from a

climbing rope in the gym. He never even smiled.)
Kelly Flynn was in the cast, too, along with several other cheerleaders who were supposed to
know how to dance because of their cheerleader
routines. Kelly is not a great dancer, in my judg-
ment. A hoofer, really. But then, who am I to
judge? I hardly know a pirouette from a do-si-do,
and I can't do either one right.

Rehearsals for *Cabaret* went well right from the
start. Although Mr. Gurzenda was officially in
charge, Donnie really ran things. He was the
choreographer as well as the star. He was very
patient with people too. He'd line them up, explain the dance steps he wanted, then run them
through the number until they got it right. He
never got upset if people blew something, and if
things weren't working out at all, he'd invent new
steps right on the spot.

When it turned out that the boys in the chorus
—there were only three—couldn't dance at all,
Donnie turned them into German soldiers and had
them march around stiffly, which is exactly what
they did when they tried to dance anyway. He
knew how to make people look good even when
they weren't, and whenever he came on stage,
even if it was just to talk to the chorus, things
perked up.

Of course, it didn't hurt that Donnie was so
good-looking. He was tall—over six feet—with
curly hair and a terrific smile. He had a dancer's

body—broad in the shoulders, trim in the waist and hips, with long, limber legs. Even when he was just walking around, he looked graceful.

The cast was mostly girls, so let's face it, they wanted to please him. Several of the girls had crushes on him and would make up dumb excuses to ask him questions or have him walk them through some steps. Even Kelly flirted with him, to my disgust, stopping to talk to him for no particular reason. But Donnie didn't seem to notice her or any other girls in that way, and he went about his work very seriously. He seemed almost indifferent to girls, and as I thought about it, I realized that I had never seen Donnie at a school dance or a party, which was odd because he probably could have had his choice of just about any girl he wanted.

We were talking about Donnie one afternoon—Kelly, who had just finished rehearsal, and Jane, who had caught up to us after a French Club meeting—and I asked them about Donnie's social life and whether he ever dated.

"What?" Kelly asked. "You on the prowl for him?" It was tough to have a conversation with Kelly about any guy. Her claws were always out. I ignored her.

"I don't think he dates anyone," Jane said.

"Well, let me tell you," Kelly said to nobody in particular, "I wouldn't mind going out with him."

"Are you kidding?" I asked. "Who's on the

prowl now? I thought you were Tom Garver's girl, true-blue, through and through."

Kelly realized she'd made a mistake.

"I was just talking 'maybe,'" she said vaguely, looking at Jane, letting her know she still claimed Tom.

"Besides," she continued, "Donnie Hamilton really won't look at girls. Not as people anyway, just as dancing partners."

I saw my chance to get Kelly back. "She should know," I said to Jane. "She's worked hard enough to get his attention in rehearsals, but he won't give her the time of day."

Kelly got mad and started to say something, and I hoped she wasn't going to say anything about *my* nonexistent social life. But at that moment Tom Garver and George Foley showed up, both with damp, freshly combed hair, probably just coming from a workout.

"Hi, girls," George said cheerily. He knew that calling us *girls* would get a rise out of me, and it did.

"Hello, *boys*," I said right back. "What manly things have you *boys* been doing?"

"What's with you?" George asked, pretending to be surprised. "What's with Wexler?"

Jane put on a frosty voice. "We'd prefer not to be called 'girls,' George, as you well know."

"Aha," George replied, doing a Groucho Marx imitation and pretending to flick a cigar. "That's

peculiar, because you sure look like goils to me."
He looked Kelly and Jane up and down, from top
to bottom, and wiggled his eyebrows. He didn't
look at me at all.

"Hi, Tom," I said, not wanting to see *that* line of
conversation go any further. "How are you doing?"

"Okay, Karen," he said quietly.

In fact, Tom was doing worse and worse. His
ego was in a downslide, and lately, Kelly hadn't
been any help to him, even acting cold to him at
times. When she had told us she was faithful to
Tom, she wasn't telling the whole truth. As a matter of fact, it was obvious that she was looking
around to see who else was available, including
Donnie Hamilton.

"How's rehearsal going?" George asked, seeing
that Tom wasn't going to say anything more.

"Great," I answered, "though you'd really have
to ask the chorus girl."

Kelly was thinking about something else and
remained silent, as if she hadn't heard me at all.

Then I said something that started off a whole
string of events, something I regretted asking for a
long time afterward.

"We were just talking about Donnie Hamilton,"
I said, "and wondering if he dates anybody or goes
out."

George gave a slow grin, and even Tom came to
life with a sort of smirk.

"Mr. Twinkletoes?" George asked. "Are you kidding? Girls aren't for him. Everybody knows about him."

"Everybody knows what?" I asked.

"*You* know," Tom said, looking over at George, who nodded. "You know," he said to me.

I was irritated. "No, I don't *know*. For Pete's sake, Tom, tell me what you think you know."

"Not *think* I know." Tom was suddenly being stubborn. "*Know.*"

"Know what?" It sounded like I'd said that before.

George tried to enlighten me. "Know," he said, "that Donnie Hamilton is a twinkletoes."

I was not enlightened. "And what does *that* mean?" To tell the truth, though, I was starting to figure it out.

Tom shrugged to George, then turned to me. "Hamilton is gay," he said. "That's all. He's gay. Everybody knows that."

"I didn't know that," Kelly said, puckering her forehead. "A cute guy like that?"

Tom shot her an angry look, but she didn't catch it.

"I don't believe that," Jane said.

"Neither do I," I added. "That's ridiculous."

"No it isn't," Tom insisted. "Why would a guy want to be a dancer anyway? That's something for girls to do, not men."

"Don't be silly," I answered back, feeling angry. "There's nothing feminine about dancing. Male dancers are really athletic."

"Oh sure," Tom said. "Oh sure." He turned to George again. "Do you remember the time sophomore year when Woodhull got Twinkletoes in gym?"

Woodhull is the football coach, with a reputation for being very tough, big on discipline. He also teaches some gym classes.

"Yeah," George said, grinning, not a pleasant grin.

"Tell them," Tom said, pointing to George, waving toward us.

George loved to tell stories when he could gather an audience. He stepped forward as if he was coming center stage.

"Well," he said to us, the women. "Here's the scene. Woodhull has us all lined up by the wall and standing at attention." He walked over to the corridor wall and came to attention himself.

"Attention?" I asked. "In gym?"

Tom nodded. "That's Woodhull's approach."

George waved him off, wanting to tell the story alone. "Every year Woodhull tries to recruit big guys to play football. He lines everybody up in gym and the ones who didn't go out for the team get asked why not."

"Oh boy" was all I could say.

"So," George continued, "Woodhull goes up to

Hamilton and pokes him in the chest." George turned to the wall and gave it a poke. " 'And what about you, mister?' Woodhull says. 'Why aren't you playing football? You're big enough.' " George faced us again. "And he is, you know, big enough."

"And what did Donnie say?" Jane asked.

George laughed. "Something funny like, 'I have other commitments, sir.' "

" 'Sir'?" I asked.

"That's Woodhull," Tom explained.

George addressed himself to the wall again. " 'Commitments!' Woodhull says. 'What kind of commitments?' " He looked over his shoulder at us. "We could see right away that Hamilton didn't want to tell him."

"But Woodhull kept after him," Tom explained.

George turned his back to the wall and came to attention. "And then Twinkletoes says something like, 'I'm interested in the dance, sir.' " George spun around and became the coach again. " 'Dance! . . . Dance? Are you telling me you would rather dance than play football?' "

"And what did *Donnie* say?" I felt it was important to emphasize his real name.

"What could he say?" George answered. " 'Yes, sir.' The whole class cracked up."

Tom was smiling at the memory even now.

"But it wasn't over yet," George said. "Woodhull goes over to him real close, stands face to face with him." George glowered at the wall from about three inches away. "And Coach says, 'You know what I think? I think that you're *afraid* to play football. I think that you're a *sissy*. And if you're not a *sissy*, I want you to tell me so right now. I want you to tell me in front of all these other men—I want you to shout it out—I want you to say that you're not a *sissy.*' "

I blazed angry, even though this had happened three years ago. "How can Woodhull get away with that? You can't say things like that to people in a school. No teacher can."

"Woodhull can," Tom said, "and does."

"So what did Donnie answer?" Jane asked. "What did he say?"

Tom gave us a vicious grin. "Nothing. Absolutely nothing."

"He just stood there," George added, "and didn't deny anything."

"And that's proof that he's a twinkletoes," Tom concluded. "It's as simple as that."

I was furious.

"Oh come on," I shouted, and I could hear my voice echo down the corridor. "That's ridiculous. That doesn't prove he's gay. There are probably a dozen reasons why he didn't say anything."

"Name one," Tom challenged.

"Well, maybe he realized that Woodhull was just trying to bait him or something like that. Or he just decided there was no point in arguing back with a person like that."

"I wouldn't have kept still," Tom said.

"Me neither," Kelly put in, as if she actually understood what it must have been like.

"Well I would have," I said. "I wouldn't have given Woodhull the satisfaction of a reply."

"But you're a girl—or, excuse me—a *woman*," George said, "and you're not expected to do those things. And besides, aren't you the one who noticed he doesn't pay attention to girls?"

"You guys are out of line." I had stopped shouting, but I was still pretty loud. "And you've got no proof, no real proof."

"We've got all the proof we need, Karen," Tom said. "And besides, who cares? It's no big deal."

George nodded.

"I care," I told them all.

"So do I," Kelly said, and Tom shot her another angry look. What was she trying to prove?

"I'll tell you what," I said. "I challenge you guys to be objective and fair about Donnie. Come to a rehearsal and watch for an hour. You'll see that dancing isn't fairy stuff. Donnie is really athletic up there. And I'm sure he isn't gay."

"I'll lay you odds he is," George said, while Tom nodded, grinning.

"Come on, George," I said, disgusted. "It's not something to clown around about or to bet on. You're not being fair to Donnie. Maybe he's just so tied up in his dancing that he doesn't have time for girls. At least come and see for yourselves."

That turned out to be the second thing I'd said that I was sorry about.

Tom and George did come to rehearsal, the very next day. They took seats way up in the back, up in the shadows, so it wasn't until part way through the rehearsal that I even realized they'd come into the auditorium. Right away I started to worry. What if Mr. Gurzenda decided to do the scene where Donnie had to pretend he was a chorus girl? If he did, with Tom and George there, it would be all over. They'd be convinced Donnie was gay. I was sorry right away that I'd asked them to come.

Fortunately, Gurzenda picked a different scene, one where the emcee and a character named Sally Bowles sing a song called "Money Makes the World Go Around." It involves a lot of dancing with the whole cast, and there were a lot of tricky lifts for Donnie to do. The rehearsal was okay, but not terrific. The cheerleader types were not so great in their timing, so there were problems with missed cues. Donnie would dance over to where he was supposed to lift one of the girls, and she wouldn't be there. Kelly was maybe the worst of the lot, because she wasn't concentrating on her steps, half the time trying to get Donnie to pay attention to her, half the time peering out into the darkness of the auditorium trying to see where Tom was sitting.

Donnie didn't let the mistakes bother him, though, and he kept on working through the number. He must have done some of those lifts three or four times with each girl, lifting her way up over his head, turning her around, and setting her down gently. He should have been absolutely exhausted, but he kept on smiling the whole time, and he didn't show any signs of wearing down.

Eventually they got through the whole number without any big mistakes and Mr. Gurzenda called it quits. I pulled the curtain shut and trotted up the aisle of the auditorium to see what Tom and George had to say.

"Hi, guys, I'm glad you could come." Mainly, though, I wasn't so much *glad* as relieved that nothing had happened.

George and Tom were slumped down in their seats, with their knees up on the backs of the seats in front of them.

"Hello, Karen," George said in a flat voice. Tom just sat there looking sour.

I was excited anyway. "So you saw. Wasn't that something?"

They both nodded slowly, but still didn't say anything.

"Did you see all those lifts?" I asked. "That's really rugged stuff, isn't it?"

Neither one spoke. I felt like I was talking to George's wall.

Kelly came up the aisle and joined us.

"I'm beat," she said, and she looked it. "Let's get out of here."

Tom and George untangled themselves and got up from their seats. We all walked into the corridor.

I was bothered that the guys were being so quiet, even surly, that they weren't getting my point, so I tried another tactic.

"Hey. Before you leave, I want you to do something. Here, Tom. You're Mr. Macho . . . Mr. Muscles . . . Mr. Football Hero. I want you to try one of those lifts. I want you to pick up Kelly and lift her over your head the way Donnie did."

"C'mon," he said. "That's stupid."

"No, you come on," I insisted. "Kelly, how much do you weigh?"

"Huh? One hundred eight." I was surprised. She looked bigger than that.

George was starting to get interested in all this. "You can press double that in the weight room. I bet you could probably lift her with one hand."

"Sure," I said. "It should be a cinch for Mr. Jock-o."

I was being kind of rough on Tom, but I didn't think he was being fair to Donnie, and I was getting sick of his gloominess anyway.

"All right," Tom said, "but it won't prove anything."

"It may prove lots of things," I answered. "Come here, Kelly."

I showed Tom where to place his hands: one in the small of her back, one right behind her knee. "Now lift her up over your head," I commanded. Tom took a deep breath and lifted. He got her up, although it was a bit awkward and he staggered a couple of steps before he got her steady.

"Ow," Kelly screamed from on high. "You're ripping the skin right off my back."

I grinned at Tom. "Now, smile like it's easy and dance a few steps."

Instead, he put her down, not at all gracefully, with a thump that made her sound like she weighed *two* hundred eight.

"Ow," Kelly cried again. "My foot."

At that moment Dr. McCollom came walking by.

"Hello, kids."

We helloed back.

"I didn't know you were interested in the dance, Tom," he said. "That's very good." And he kept on walking.

Tom said nothing, but turned red out of anger or embarrassment or maybe both.

"You see," I said happily. "Dr. McCollom thinks it's okay for boys to dance. There's nothing gay or queer or wrong with it at all." I gestured over to Kelly, who was sitting on the floor rubbing her ankle. "And you can see that it's not all that easy."

Tom turned to me, angry. "That's not the point, Karen."

"What isn't? Of course it is. Didn't you see what Donnie was doing out there?"

"*That,*" Tom said, "is the point. I saw."

"Saw what?" Here we went again. "Were you really looking or did you have your mind made up in advance?"

"Oh, I looked all right," Tom answered, "and I saw exactly what was going on."

I was exasperated. "And what was that? What, exactly, did you see going on?"

"We saw what he was doing with the girls," George said.

"Let Tom talk, will you?" I said. "I want to know what he saw."

Tom shrugged. "What he was doing with the girls."

"And what was that?" I'm no dumbo, but I couldn't figure out what he was saying.

"The way he was touching them," Tom explained.

"Touching them?"

"Come on, Karen," George said, "do we have to spell it out for you?"

"I guess so," I shouted, "because what you're saying makes no sense."

Tom shook his head slowly. "If you want me to say it, he was . . . copping a feel."

"Copping a . . ." Suddenly I realized what he was talking about. "You mean when he was danc-

ing with the girls you think he was getting something off them?"

He nodded yes, and I could see he was serious.
I couldn't be. I broke into hysterical laughter.
Almost screaming laughter. The kind I hate in
other people.

"Do you realize," I said between bursts of gig-
gling, "how ridiculous that sounds? Yesterday you
were accusing him of being gay. Now you're
claiming he was fooling around with the chorus
girls. You've totally contradicted yourself."

Tom shrugged. "I saw what I saw."

I stopped laughing. Now I was angry, but I
tried to keep my voice quiet and in control.

"I was backstage, you know, and I saw the rehearsal at close range. I know what he was doing
and not doing. For crying out loud, he has to
touch the girls to dance with them."

"Not the way he was touching them," Tom insisted. "And the thing that got me was that he
kept making them do it over and over again, like
he wasn't getting enough."

"That's a rehearsal!" I exploded. "That's what
it's for, to do things over and over to get them
right."

"He was getting it, all right." Tom leered at me.

"Oh for heaven's sake," I said. "Kelly." She was
still on the floor rubbing her ankle, not really paying a lot of attention to us. "Will you talk to this

jerk? Tell him what Donnie was doing in rehearsal."

"Doing?"

"This dumbbell"—I waved in the direction of Tom—"thinks Donnie was getting away with something. Was he? Was he touching you somehow?"

Kelly thought. "Well, no, not really."

"You see?" I said.

Unfortunately, Kelly wasn't through thinking. "Of course, sometimes if he would slip a little bit . . ."

"Yeah?" Tom asked, sensing something coming.

"Well, I mean, he might get a little bit of you, like your butt, or something." She gave a flirtatious wink. "But what the heck, that's show business."

I could see what she was up to. Anybody could. She wanted to make Tom jealous. I know she was lying, or hinting about something that never happened. I know Donnie hadn't grabbed her. He was too good a dancer to do that, and he wasn't interested in Kelly anyway. But what Kelly had said was enough for Tom. He didn't need any more evidence in his mood.

"He needs to be taught a lesson," he said quietly.

I was worried. "Oh, come on. You sound like something out of a gangster movie."

"He's right, Karen," George said. "We can't let him get away with that."

"Are you crazy, George? Do you believe this too?"

"It doesn't matter so much what *I* believe. Tom is my friend. I've got to look out for his interests."

"His interests?" I was shouting again. "This *interest?*" I waved in Kelly's direction and ran out of words, but they knew what I meant, and the three of them stood there, facing me: Tom angry and even vicious, Kelly catty and jealous, and George, for some reason, going along with them. Where was Jane? I needed a friend.

They turned away from me and began walking down the corridor. Kelly was hobbling on her ankle, leaning on Tom and George. The next thing you knew, she'd be claiming that it was Donnie, not Tom, who had hurt her.

"It's your male ego that's the problem," I called after Tom. "I think you're worried that Donnie's more of a man than you are. I think you're jealous of him."

They didn't act as if they'd even heard me, but I know they had. I think I was right, too, but that made three things I probably shouldn't have said.

Everything came to a head the next day at rehearsal. Tom and George showed up again and sat in the same seats, half-hidden in the darkness. I didn't have a chance to talk to them before rehearsal, not that I really wanted to. I thought they were acting like a couple of creeps. In fact, it was worse than that; they were really being scary. They reminded me of the Gestapo in *Cabaret,* always hanging around and watching, just waiting to catch somebody doing something they thought was wrong.

On that day, Mr. Gurzenda had decided to run us through a rehearsal in simple costumes and makeup, just to get the feel of things. Later we'd rent costumes from a theatrical supply house in Cleveland, but for now, people just scrounged up whatever they could. The chorus girls all came in gym shorts and brightly colored T-shirts, and we gave them heavy makeup: dark red lips, heavily rouged cheeks, and lots of eye shadow and mascara. Our Gestapos showed up in old Boy Scout uniforms, and a couple of the guys had on high-topped hiking boots to give themselves a military look. Donnie Hamilton wore a striped tank-top and over that an old tuxedo jacket. We made him up in whiteface plus lipstick, with black lines drawn around his eyes. He looked partly like a clown, partly like a ghost, which was perfect for the part.

The rehearsal was super, and I could see that just these simple costumes made a big difference in how kids got into their parts. Everybody danced and sang better than ever, and we could get a real idea of what the play was going to be like. I could feel in my bones that it was going to be a smash. You can tell about those things.

I got so absorbed watching that I almost forgot about Tom and George sitting at the back. But after Mr. Gurzenda had wished the class a good evening, and while I was pulling the curtain, I looked back and was surprised to see them coming down the aisle. They were coming fast, practically marching, with Tom in the lead, George following. They jumped from the auditorium floor to the stage and disappeared behind the curtains on the far side. The boys' dressing room is downstairs on that side, so I knew where they were headed.

I also figured I had to catch up with them before they reached the dressing room, where I couldn't go. I charged across the stage and down a short flight of cement stairs, hanging on to the railing to keep from falling. I caught up with them in a small storage room at the bottom of the stairs, the place where we have lockers to keep the props and costumes. By the time I got there, though, Tom had cornered Donnie among the lockers. George was standing nearby, keeping watch, and Donnie was glancing back and forth between George and Tom as if trying to figure out what was happening. I could see that Tom had worked himself into a rage; he was pale, almost as white as Donnie's makeup, and he was shaking with anger. Donnie just looked puzzled.

"Okay, Twinkletoes," Tom said with a sneer that made him look really ugly. "It's time for you to pay the price."

"Hey," I yelled. "What's wrong with you? Get out of here. You can't do this."

Donnie looked over and saw me, and he looked even more puzzled, probably over what I was doing there and what I was hollering about. He looked strange, because even though his makeup was sort of clownlike, he had become very serious.

"Get out of here, Karen," Tom said quietly, holding his anger in. "Get her out of here, George."

George grabbed me by the wrist and started to push me back toward the stairs. I wrenched my arm away, giving myself a good wrist burn in the process, but I was furious.

"Get your hands off me, George," I snarled, and he backed off, surprised, maybe even a little scared. "Stop this!" I said to him. "Make him stop."

George shook his head. He was stubborn; he wasn't going to do anything; he was on Tom's side no matter what. Dumb loyalty.

Tom ignored us, and he continued looking straight at Donnie, trying to scare him or maybe psych him out.

"Come on, Twinkletoes," Tom said, raising his fists in a boxer's stance and starting to move in for the fight. "You can't dance your way out of this."

Then Tom took a swing at Donnie, a big knock-out kind of punch. Tom is strong from sports, and he could really hurt Donnie. I was ready to scream for help.

But Donnie stood his ground, and as the punch

came, he casually leaned way back on his heels—
limber, like a dancer—and drew his head out of
the way. Tom missed him by at least six inches
and looked foolish, like a baseball batter when
he's swung hard at a pitch and missed.

Then Donnie did an amazing thing. He actually
did dance his way out of it. As Tom's fist flew past,
Donnie gave a pantomime face of surprise, his
mouth puckered up and his eyes open wide. Then
he shuffled his feet in a soft-shoe step, and his
whole body started flopping around like a rag doll,
his head wagging back and forth. Next he raised
his hands and made them into fists, but with the
knuckles turned out like an old-time prizefighter,
and he bobbed around in the corner where Tom
had backed him, tapping out a rhythm on the
lockers with his knuckles and keeping time with
his feet. It was very funny, and despite all the
tension, I started to smile. Looking at George
Foley, I could see that deep down in his heart he
thought it was funny too. It was his kind of humor.

Tom didn't think it was funny, though. He
watched for a moment and then slowly lowered
his hands and turned away from Donnie and
started walking for the stairs. Then, suddenly, he
swung a punch from his waist right into the nearest locker, actually caving in the door and tipping
the locker over against the wall. It had to have
hurt his hand, but he didn't even grimace as he
stalked to the stairs.

George looked over at me, then walked around me to the stairs, giving me a wide berth. I shook my head as he went by. He should have known better.

Donnie stopped dancing and watched them go. I think he still had no real idea what was going on.

I was going to talk to him, to say something to him by way of explanation, to explain that they thought he was gay but then they thought he was too free with the girls but that Kelly Flynn had helped to set the whole thing up and that I didn't know or care whether he was gay or a masher but I was ashamed of my friends. Fortunately, before I could start, a voice from the dressing room door interrupted us.

"Mr. Hamilton," it said. "I wonder if you and I might go out for a bite to eat?"

Donnie and I looked over into the shadows.

"And," the Burg-O-Rama Man continued, moving toward us, "I'd like you to bring along your friends."

Donnie looked up the stairs in the direction George and Tom had taken. Now he *really* looked puzzled.

The Burg-O-Rama Man chuckled. It was like a TV actor's laugh—rich, confident.

"No, I don't mean those two," he said. "I mean the cast of *Cabaret*."

◆ ◆ ◆

OPENING SHOT: A Burg-O-Rama logo fills the screen against a black background.

ANNOUNCER: Burg-O-Rama would like to introduce . . .

SHOT: Logotype vanishes, leaving a black screen.

ANNOUNCER: Donnie Hamilton of Crawford High School.

MUSIC: Drum roll and cymbal crash.

SHOT: Donnie's head pops up in the blackness. He is wearing his *Cabaret* whiteface. He mugs at the camera: a face of wide-eyed surprise, then a wink.

ANNOUNCER: The faculty says Donnie is the finest actor and dancer ever to go to Crawford High School.

SHOT: Lights come on and the camera zooms back to reveal the *Cabaret* cast lined up behind him, frozen in dance positions.

MUSIC: Burg-O-Rama theme with theater orchestra, strong beat.

SHOT: Donnie swirls into action and the cast starts doing one of its routines.

ANNOUNCER: Donnie plans to pursue a career as a professional dancer.

SHOTS: Freeze frames of Donnie in motion: jumps, lifts, spins, kicks.

ANNOUNCER: He'll be pursuing his studies on a Burg-O-Rama scholarship.

SHOT: Close-up of Donnie's face, no makeup. Camera backs away revealing that the background is now the Burg-O-Rama restaurant. Cast members can be seen sitting in the booths.

ANNOUNCER: Donnie and his friends know that when they're through rehearsing, the place to go for a snack or a meal is their local Burg-O-Rama.

SHOT: The cast members turn to face the camera. Some rise and stand; others sit on benches, tables, and ledges. The screen is filled with kids. Foreground: Donnie raises his arms like a symphony conductor.

MUSIC: The cast sings, orchestra softly playing in the background:

> *Burg-O-Rama's a friendly spot,*
> *To get good food, both cold and hot.*
> *Take your friends out for a treat.*
> *Burg-O-Rama's the place to eat.*

SHOT: Donnie turns. His conductor's waving becomes a wave at the camera. Kids behind him wave. Picture fades and is replaced by Burg-O-Rama logo, which shrinks to the upper-left corner, followed by announcement:

A promotional fee has been paid to the Crawford City, Ohio, Public Schools and to Donald Hamilton by the Burg-O-Rama Foundation, a division of Trimble Enterprises, Inc.

◆ ◆ ◆

I thought Donnie's was probably the best commercial in the whole series. It was the only one that seemed completely true to life and not somehow distorting the star. Of course, much of that is due to Donnie and the fact that he is a good actor. I mean, the commercial may have been real, but it was still acting. But it was real as far as the acting went, if you can follow all that.

Anyhow, I was pleased that Donnie was chosen. I thought he deserved it, and picking him to be on national television really made his dancing seem all right, that there was not something unnatural about a boy who liked to dance. I'm sure that over his high school years Donnie probably caught a lot of teasing from people like Tom and George and Coach Woodhull who just didn't understand what he was doing and had no understanding of people who weren't jock types. It was good that Donnie was picked.

Although I was happy about Donnie, I was really unhappy about things with the Power Mongers—at least with Kelly, Tom, and George. I tried to talk to Jane about it the next day, dragging her into the *Tiger Eye* office for privacy just before school began. She'd heard about the fight —or the nonfight—but I told her the whole thing again, since I had been the only witness except for George and the Burg-O-Rama Man.

"Why would Tom do something like that?" I asked her. "I mean, why would he do that? He didn't have to be that way, and it's just not like Tom."

Jane was way down. "I guess he's just under a lot of pressure," she said quietly.

"Pressure!" I exploded. "Are you kidding me? He's not under any pressure. Half the senior class is under more pressure than he is, and they don't go around trying to beat people up."

"Well," she said, "I know it's hard to understand. But Tom just doesn't feel good—happy—anymore." She didn't look at me.

I pounded my fist dramatically on the editor's desk, making a stack of papers slide off on the floor. "Doesn't feel good? Isn't happy? Come on, Jane, that's no excuse. You're making excuses for him because you love him."

She looked up at me and I could see that she was suddenly angry. "Come on yourself, Karen." She was practically shouting at me, and Jane almost never raises her voice. "Don't be so self-righteous and know-it-all. You think it's all so simple with Tom that you can judge him. Well it isn't. It isn't simple at all, so why don't you just butt out?" She put her head down on my desk and began to cry.

I felt terrible and reached out to touch her on the shoulder, but she sensed me coming.

"Get out of here, will you?" she choked out. "Just get out and leave me alone."

So I got out. Of my own newspaper office. I just got out and went to classes and felt rotten all day, thinking about what Jane had said about me being "self-righteous." I had thought I was trying to help, but she just thought I was butting in. I didn't know what to do or think.

I did take her advice and butt out of Tom's affairs, though. I just stayed away from him. Kelly, too, because I thought she had acted like a complete bubblehead. And self-righteous or not, I was angry with George too. I just didn't understand why a guy who was basically nice and fun-loving would stick up for somebody like Tom, who I thought had turned into a complete creep. I couldn't avoid George completely because of newspaper business, but I couldn't be close friends with him anymore. I cut him the one way I knew best: I stopped laughing at his jokes.

Jane and I made up after about a week. I think our friendship was too deep to be ruined. I told her I was sorry about being so hard on her about Tom, and she apologized for snapping at me. We hugged, and we've been back on track ever since.

But neither of us will forget that time, I'm sure.

So the whole business with Donnie really meant the end of the Power Mongers—we were never together again as a group after that. I felt guilty, to some extent. I know, or have been taught, that friends are people you stick by, no matter what happens to them or what they do. But also friends change, and people change, and sometimes not in the best ways. Sometimes, too, you have to draw a line when things happen, and after Tom and George and Kelly were so terrible about Donnie, that was a line I had to draw.

CHAPTER

6

The time that the Burg-O-Rama Man would be spending with us was drawing to a close. He had been at Crawford High School for almost a month, and four of the five people to be in the television commercials had already been chosen. The kids were used to seeing him around school, and we hardly even noticed the Big Fella with his cameras walking about the halls. Although there had been a lot of curiosity in the early days about who would be picked for the commercials, there was less and less excitement each time a name was announced. I think a lot of people just don't think they had a chance so they didn't care anymore.

But I figured there was enough interest left that the Burg-O-Rama Man would be a good subject for a story for the paper. I realized that nobody knew very much about him, except maybe that he had a lot of nice clothes, but I wondered what he thought about us—the people of Crawford.

So one day at the very end of March found me using my lunch hour doing something unusual: cleaning up the *Tiger Eye* office. Papers had piled up all year—on the window ledge, on my desk, even on the extra chair, the chair on which my interviewee, the Burg-O-Rama Man, would sit. Most of the stuff was old, so I just dumped it, not even checking to see if it ought to be filed away. I had just finished up this work when there was a knock on the door.

"Come on in," I said, though the office is so small I could have reached right over and opened the door.

The Burg-O-Rama Man came in. He was dressed as usual in a suit, this one light tan—and he had on a pale yellow shirt and a brown tie with gold stripes. Everything was right in place and color-matched, which was his style. I was embarrassed about the office, but he didn't seem to notice it, not even checking the chair for dust before he sat down.

"Hello," he said, "nice to see you again."

"Thanks for coming," I replied. "Nice to see you again too."

Enough of the small talk. I figured he was busy, so I started right in on the list of questions I had prepared in my head.

"You've been an observer here all month," I said, "but as I thought about it, I realized that nobody knows exactly what you think. I'd like to find out."

"Certainly," he said, spreading his hands. "I'll answer as best I can."

"Well, I guess the big thing everybody wants to know is how you actually go about picking the different people for the Burg-O-Rama commercials. How do you decide? Do you do it by yourself?"

"No, I don't do it alone," he answered, "though I make the basic recommendations. The final decisions are made by a group of people in New York. I've been flying back to meet with them once each week."

"So that's where you are when you're not around school?"

"There, and at home in New Jersey, taking the weekend off." He smiled at me. "I don't work seven days, you know, and school's closed on weekends."

I thought about asking him what he did on weekends. Did he have a family or anything like that? But I decided that would be too nosy. Instead, I stayed with the commercials.

"But how do you go about deciding on the recommendations? I mean, is there a set way to it?"

"To some extent," he said, shifting his chair and

trying to make a little more room for himself in the office. "But it's as much art as science. As you said, I'm an observer. I watch people around school, and when I see someone who seems to have that special spark, I tell Ken Deitrick, and he gets some footage on that person."

I nodded.

"In a way, Karen," he continued, "my job is a lot like yours."

"Huh?"

"As I see it, you're an observer, too, through your *Tiger Eye*. You look around for special people, special stories, and when you recognize them you do an article about them. In a way, you and I are in the same business."

"I don't know," I said, because I didn't quite see the connection. "Anyway, you said you shoot some film?"

"Right. Every few days, after he's shot a couple of reels, Ken Deitrick and I sit down with a projector and screen all the takes. Often we'll see some material that has potential."

"Material." That sounded kind of impersonal to me. "Do you mean pictures of people?"

"Exactly. Then Ken edits all the material we have on a given person into a single film clip. It might be just two or three minutes, but it will show the person in all aspects of his day."

Or *hers*, I said to myself.

"Next I take the film to New York, show it to my

editorial group, and if they like what I've selected, I notify the person he's been chosen."

"Or *she*," I said aloud.

"Or she," he agreed.

"Have all your recommendations been accepted? Do they ever reject your ideas?" Somehow I couldn't imagine *anybody* rejecting one of the Burg-O-Rama Man's ideas.

"Not so much reject," he said, "as not accept."

"I beg your pardon?"

"Ken has put together film on seventeen people so far, and of those, four have been chosen. We have two or three others that have potential, that we might use as backup, but the rest were not usable for one reason or another."

"Rejected," I said.

"No, just not accepted."

I didn't exactly see the difference, but it wasn't worth worrying about.

"I don't suppose you could tell me the names of those people? The ones who *didn't* get picked? It would make a great story: 'SO NEAR, YET SO FAR: CLOSE ENCOUNTERS WITH STARDOM.'"

He laughed. "You know the answer to that one, of course. I'm afraid that would create hard feelings toward Burg-O-Rama, and we wouldn't want that."

Dead end, so I changed directions.

"What about Crawford City itself? How did it get picked?"

"Actually by a similar process. I observed a number of towns and cities in mid-America—in Ohio, Indiana, Illinois, and Iowa—and Ken put together film packages on each one, to which I added a report on whether I thought the city would be receptive to us. Then I recommended my top choice and two backups to the planning group."

"Crawford was top choice? Not one of the backups?" I wondered if he would actually tell me if we were second or third choice.

"Crawford came out number one." I gave him my quizzical look. "Absolutely," he emphasized. "Everything is very photogenic here. The school. The town square. Even the students in the school. Everything in Crawford has that typical American image that we wanted to project."

There he was talking "typical" again. And all this business about "material" and "images" was bothering me. Maybe my job was a little like the Burg-O-Rama Man's, but I never thought about my stories that way. I fiddled with my note pad, pretending to write something down, but actually thinking of how to ask a new question.

"It seems to me," I finally said, "that a lot of what you are doing is more concerned with images than anything else."

He looked at me and tilted his head to one side. I'd made him suspicious. He waited for me to say more.

"The other day," I said, "somebody was talking to me about you." Actually nobody had talked to me, but it seemed better to put these words into somebody else's mouth. "And she said, 'Why is the Burg-O-Rama Man doing all this stuff about typical kids in a typical town? We know that all they're doing is selling junk food.' "

I suddenly realized that I had called him "the Burg-O-Rama Man" to his face. Hardly a polite thing to do. I forgot where I was going and stammered. "And . . . uh . . ."

He understood what was bothering me.

"It's all right to call me that," he said. "I know that's the name you have for me. In fact, I told my girl friend about it and she was amused. She had a T-shirt made up for me."

Well, there was some information about his private life. A "girl friend," not a wife. But I absolutely could not picture the Burg-O-Rama Man wearing a T-shirt.

"What did it say?" I asked, feeling reassured to the point of being nosy.

"I'm not certain I should say."

"Oh, it's okay," I said. "I can handle it."

"I don't doubt that," he answered, "but this is not something I'd want in the school paper."

"No problem. Let's make it off the record. For my curiosity alone. You can trust me."

"It says"—and he paused for a long moment—"THE BURG-O-RAMA MAN DOES IT WITH RELISH."

And he looked away, a little embarrassed. It was the first time I'd ever seen him uncomfortable.

I loved it and laughed, though I still couldn't imagine him wearing a T-shirt or with a girl friend who would give him one that said something like that. I pictured him leading a life like someone in a wine commercial—having dinner by candlelight, him in one of his suits, her dressed in clothes right out of a fashion magazine. Then I realized I'd probably been unfair to him, that I'd had a false image of him. He probably sat around on weekends with his girl friend, both of them in jeans, drinking beer like anybody else.

He interrupted my thoughts. "But you raised the issue of junk food." Suddenly he was the Burg-O-Rama Man again, all business, and I figured that I'd probably heard all I was going to about his private life.

"I know you and your classmates studied that in Mr. Walton's biology class. I couldn't help overhearing some of what that student—"

"Russ Moffett?"

"—Russ Moffett was saying about fast-food chains." He leaned forward in his chair. "I want you to know, Karen—and this is *for* the record—that as I've said repeatedly, Burg-O-Rama is *not* a junk food outfit. Everything we sell is perfectly legal. We abide strictly by federal regulations. We do not adulterate our food with artificial materials the way some fast-food places do."

Materials, he had said, now meaning chemicals, not people.

"But what about the case in Maryland Russ told us about?" I asked. "Where Burg-O-Rama was putting soybeans into the hamburger meat."

"Our attorneys tell us we were perfectly in the clear on that." He smiled at me, though it was a smile of confidence rather than friendliness. "However, because the people in Maryland were concerned, Burg-O-Rama has voluntarily refrained from using any more soy product. That's something your friend Russ Moffett *didn't* tell you."

If it was legal, why were they going to stop doing it? The whole thing sounded funny to me.

He read my thoughts. "We're service-oriented, Karen, and we must be deeply conscious of our image with the general public. If our clients don't want something done, we won't do it, even if it is technically legal."

Clients? Was that another of his words for *people?* I chewed on my pencil.

"So," I said, "you stick by your claim that Burg-O-Rama stuff is '100% natural.' "

"Absolutely," he said with great conviction, looking hard at me. "Absolutely." After a few seconds I had to look away, down at my notes.

He leaned back and broke the silence. "If we could go off the record again, I would agree with you and your classmates if you said there's a lot of sugar, fat, and carbohydrate in our products. That's true and I don't deny it."

If he didn't deny it, I wondered, why didn't he want it in the paper? But he continued before I could ask.

"Man cannot live by milkshakes alone," he said, smiling away at me.

Was he trying to charm his way out?

"Or woman, either," I insisted.

He nodded. "I'd be the first to admit that if you ate only at Burg-O-Rama, your diet wouldn't necessarily be complete and balanced. However, our food is perfectly all right for you. It is certainly not junk food. And that statement is one I wish you'd print, because your fellow students should be convinced of it."

I wasn't really convinced myself, but I was pretty sure he was sincere, and I don't think he was lying to me. Or if he was lying, I certainly couldn't think up a question that would trick him. He was too quick and polished for me. So I changed the topic, leading up to another question I wanted to ask him, a favor really.

"You know, at this time of the year it's hard to get interesting news into the paper."

"I see," he said, but there was a question mark in his voice that said he didn't understand why I'd said that.

"But sometimes I can get a real scoop and print

something in the paper before it happens, like an announcement of something coming up."

He nodded. Now he was starting to guess, but he wasn't going to say anything yet.

"You still have to announce the star for one more commercial, right?"

He nodded again.

"How about telling me in advance who the last person will be and letting me announce it in the *Tiger Eye*? That would be a terrific scoop. I could use a headline like, FINAL BURGER STAR REVEALED INSIDE, and I could run a story on how you came to choose this last person."

He pushed his chair back and it hit the doorknob with a bang. He laughed, that TV actor's laugh I'd heard from him before.

I didn't think it was that funny or ridiculous an idea. "I wouldn't leak the story," I told him, thinking maybe he was afraid I'd blab it around. "I promise, nobody would know. I'd even proofread the galleys myself, so nobody would have a chance to see the story but me."

I know I was begging a little bit, but this was something I wanted. It was maybe the last chance of my senior year to get people excited about the *Tiger Eye*.

"I don't know," the Burg-O-Rama Man said slowly. "That would present some complications. Because, you see, I have to get a person's agreement to be in the commercial before I go ahead and announce his name."

"Or hers." I'd teach him to remember that yet.

"Or hers." He actually winked at me. The guy was a charmer, and I was flustered again. But I wasn't going to let him get away with a wink, so I hung on.

"Well, then," I said, "maybe you could get his or her agreement and then I could talk to him or her and get them to give me an exclusive interview." All those *his* and *hers* were awkward, but I had to get them in.

"Maybe," he answered, "but I can imagine that in the case of the particular person selected for this last commercial, it could lead to some complications for you and your paper."

So he knew who the last person was going to be. I *had* to get him to let me in on it.

"It can't be all that complicated," I said. "There's got to be some way to work it out."

He shot me a great big smile, and this time it was a natural one, not a businessman's smile. If his girl friend was interested in cute guys with a terrific set of teeth, she'd found one.

"Well, it's certainly too complicated to go into here," he said, still beaming away at me. "So why don't we go over to Burg-O-Rama and discuss it over lunch?"

• • •

I'm sorry to say that it took me a while to figure out what was going on. When the Burg-O-Rama Man said he wanted to take me to lunch, I figured he just wanted to continue our conversation in a better place. I was packing up my notebook and pencil when he stopped me.

"You won't need that," he said. "You're the one."

"The one what?"

"The focus of the last commercial. The 'star' as you like to put it."

I thought he was joking. "Yeah, right," I said. "Hollywood, here I come." I fluffed up the back of my hair like an actress or model.

And then, quietly, but in a deep voice, he said, "Karen." That's all, just "Karen."

At that moment, I knew he was serious and my stomach dropped away. I had one of those unreal moments when I didn't know quite who I was, like I was watching what was going on as if I was outside my own body.

"Why me?" was all I could say.

"You may not have known it," he said, "but I've been watching you almost from the first day I arrived here." My stomach dropped even further. That was weird, to think that somebody had been watching you for a long time and you didn't even know it. "And so has Kenneth Deitrick, who has quite a bit of footage on you."

"But why me?" was all I could say again. "I can

think of a hundred kids who would be better."

"I don't think so," he said, "and neither do the people in New York who saw your film clips." If there was anyplace left for my stomach to go, it would have dropped again, and I had a sickening image of a bunch of men, all in suits like the Burg-O-Rama Man, sitting around a polished table and watching movies of me.

"The fact is, Karen," he continued, "you're a very interesting person. When I said earlier that you're a kind of observer like I am, I didn't just mean for your newspaper."

"You didn't?"

"You're an observer of people, too, and you have a good eye for spotting people who are interesting or unusual, or who need a friend."

I guess I could see what he was talking about, but I shrugged anyway.

"Certainly," he said. "You're a good friend to some fascinating people—people like Mary Costello and Donnie Hamilton and Jeff Leuders, the people I've already chosen for the commercials. You're the one who can tie it all together for us."

"But," I complained, "you said before that you're looking for somebody with spark. You want somebody like Jane Heath . . . or"—I had to say it—"even Kelly Flynn. Not somebody blah like me."

"You underrate yourself," he said. "Trust me to spot the right person. You have plenty of spark.

And remember, I've seen your image on film. You'll be pleasantly surprised when you see the clips."

I shook my head, but he kept on talking.

"We're thinking of using a phrase to describe you: the 'be-everywhere, do-everything' person."

I made a face. I would be embarrassed at that.

"You're editor of the paper, good student, sports enthusiast, active in extracurricular activities, and—"

"Yeah?" I wasn't so embarrassed that I didn't want to hear more of this.

"—you're filled with enthusiasm for life, and it shows. You're exactly the kind of person we want for the commercial, the kind of person to represent our products. Wait till you see that film."

Well, at that point, I had no idea what to think, and all sorts of thoughts rushed through my head. I know that I had doubts about Burg-O-Rama and what they were doing, and one side of me believed they were just a junk food outfit, and I wondered whether I should let them use me to sell their stuff. But the other side of me said, "Who cares?" It would be terrific to be on television coast to coast, recognized by all kinds of people. I wanted to see my image on film, and I wished the Burg-O-Rama Man could show me the clips right there on the spot.

But what if he wasn't being straight with me? He was so worried about images and appearances, what if he wasn't being straight? Or what if he was wrong about me just as I'd been wrong about him and his girl friend? Or what if he was picking me just because I was plain old Karen Wexler, Ohio girl, Miss Typical U.S.A.?

I thought about my friends and what they would say. Tom and Kelly I couldn't even call my friends anymore, but I knew what they would think. They would be jealous, and Kelly would maybe even make up lies about why I got chosen instead of somebody like her. George, I guessed, would be okay. He might be jealous, but he would have fun with the whole thing and probably offer to be my agent for fifty percent or something.

Jane is the one I really wanted to talk to about it. As I thought, however, I figured I knew pretty much what she would say—she'd tell me to make up my own mind, that we'd still be friends no matter what decision I made.

I actually didn't think all that much about money. I knew that it would be a big help in paying my way through college, but I guess I worried a little that if I took the money, I would have somehow sold a part of myself to Burg-O-Rama and just become part of their image making.

I must have thought for a long time, and the Burg-O-Rama Man just sat there. Then he brought me back.

"Shall we go to lunch now?" he said, smiling.

And at that moment, for some reason I thought about peanut butter. I thought about peanut butter spread on honey wheat bread: the peanut butter sandwich that was sitting in my desk drawer along with an apple. I was thinking about the brown bag lunch I had brought from home. It wasn't much, but it was my own.

"Thanks," I said slowly. "But I guess . . . I think I'll just have my lunch here."

The Burg-O-Rama Man looked at me hard for a moment. I thought he was angry with me or maybe he hadn't understood what I meant, and I was about to try to explain to him more exactly just why I didn't think I could do the ad.

As I started to speak, he broke into a smile.

"Wait till they hear about this in New York," he said, and I started to worry that maybe I would cause some problems for him.

"Karen Wexler," he said, rising and putting out his hand. "It has been a pleasure." We shook hands, and then the Burg-O-Rama Man, Mr. Robert Leseney, turned and left the room.

◆ ◆ ◆

OPENING SHOT: The front steps of Crawford High School, filmed from a distance. Two people are standing on the steps. The camera zooms in slowly and they are seen to be a boy and girl. They are talking, their backs to the camera.

ANNOUNCER: Burg-O-Rama wants you to meet Crawford High School's "be-everywhere, do-everything" girl.

SHOT: Camera zooms in more, focusing on the girl, who turns to face the camera.

ANNOUNCER: Her name is Kelly Flynn.

SHOT: Kelly gives the cameraman a great smile, while in the background, slightly out of focus, Tom Garver turns around and looks at Kelly admiringly.

MUSIC: Burg-O-Rama theme, school hymn motif.

ANNOUNCER: Kelly is a good student in school.

SHOT: Kelly and Tom walking into the school library, holding hands, carrying books in their free hands.

ANNOUNCER: Kelly is an active participant in her classes.

SHOTS: Kelly in her carrot costume, pointing to a heading on the chalkboard that says, "Vitamin A." Talking with Robert Walton at his desk. Waving her hand in class to catch a teacher's attention.

ANNOUNCER: She is a school leader . . .

SHOTS: Kelly up on a ladder in jeans, decorating the gym. In her cheerleader uniform running front and center at a pep rally.

ANNOUNCER: . . . sports enthusiast . . .

MUSIC: Fight song motif.

SHOTS: Kelly leading the crowd in a cheer. In a

mob of people after a basketball game. Hugging a player.

ANNOUNCER: . . . active in extracurricular activities.

SHOT: Kelly on stage in costume with Donnie Hamilton.

ANNOUNCER: Above all, Kelly Flynn is a good friend to a great many people at Crawford High School.

SHOTS: A series of images of Kelly with students in the lunchroom, in the hallways, huddled with other cheerleaders.

ANNOUNCER: Kelly and her friends know . . .

SHOT: The Burg-O-Rama restaurant packed with kids, most of them wearing Crawford orange and black.

ANNOUNCER: . . . that Burg-O-Rama is *the* place in Crawford City to go for a snack or a meal.

SHOT: Kelly coming through the front door of Burg-O-Rama, giving a big wave to the gang— everyone looks up.

ANNOUNCER: And if Burg-O-Rama is the place to go in a typical American town like Crawford City . . .

SHOTS: Freeze frames of kids eating a variety of Burg-O-Rama products.

ANNOUNCER: . . . it's the place to go in your town too.

SHOT: Close-up of Kelly, struggling politely with a

french fry. She winks at the camera. Freeze.
MUSIC: Burg-O-Rama theme swells to finish.
SHOT: Logotype fills the screen, then shrinks to
upper-left corner. Message appears:

> A promotional fee has been paid to the
> Crawford City, Ohio, Public Schools and to
> Kelly Flynn by the Burg-O-Rama Foun-
> dation, a division of Trimble Enterprises,
> Inc.

◆　◆　◆

Nobody in school ever learned that I had been
offered a chance to do one of the commercials.
The Burg-O-Rama Man didn't tell anyone, and I
certainly didn't, not even Jane. When I learned
that Kelly had been picked in my place, I felt
angry at first, and I felt angry again when I saw
the ad and realized that the Burg-O-Rama Man
had taken my slogan— the "be-everywhere, do-
everything" girl—and applied it to Kelly. As I
thought about it, though, I realized that the
slogan applied to her in her own way, and I still
had to admit that, with all her flash, Kelly was
probably a better choice—even though she was
second choice—and I stopped being angry.

As soon as I stopped being mad, I had a chance
to think about myself and wonder. I have always
seen myself as an outsider, a kind of loner, an
observer—like the Burg-O-Rama Man said—

somebody who knows what's going on and sees it at a distance. But the Burg-O-Rama Man had told me I was somebody at the center of things, and I liked it—I liked thinking of myself as an active person who is a "be-everywhere, do-everything" person. Not like Kelly, of course. Not like Kelly, who always *has* to be at the center of attention and spends all her time trying to get there. Now I understand that I don't have to be just an observer if I don't want to be, and maybe I'm not.

About the Author

STEPHEN TCHUDI grew up in Naugatuck, Connecticut. He is a graduate of Hamilton College, Clinton, New York, and holds master's and doctoral degrees from Northwestern University. He currently teaches English at Michigan State University.

Mr. Tchudi lives in Okemos, Michigan, with his wife and four children. He is the president-elect of the National Council of Teachers of English. This is his first young adult novel.